My Years in Triumph
A Search for the Lost Utopia

An Interpretation of Events by

Carl Massaro

Ideas into Books®
WESTVIEW
Kingston Springs, Tennessee

ISBN 978-1-62880-255-9

First edition, May 2015

Ideas into Books®
W E S T V I E W
P.O. Box 605
Kingston Springs, TN 37082
www.publishedbywestview.com

A grateful thanks to Patric House, The Idaho Historical Society, and Wendy Collins for photos. I would also like to thank Victoria E Mitchel for her work on the History of the Triumph Mine.

Preface

In my first book, *Bright White*, I told a tale of the golden years of the Wood River Mining district and Sun Valley. It was a time when men saw no limits , except the high cloud layers that gasoline engines could carry them to. Now let's fast forward to "The age of Aquarius." This is the story of the next generation after WW2: the children of the winners, destined and dedicated to making the world a better place. No more would men be burdened with the struggle for material wealth, no longer would governments be burdened with the problems of a bi-metal backed currency. But that's another tale. This is the story of my generation, the children who fled the costal areas of America to start new, away from the judgmental eyes of their parents, fresh from the colleges, soaked with opinion. This is the story of "Triumph Inc" and other things.

I dedicate this book to Gifford Pinchot, Americas first forester, To Milton Harr, the father of Idaho's New Age movement, and to Earl Holding, for keeping the world's best ski mountain open , through good times and bad .

There's money in junk…

If you're going to make a change in this world, you need to begin in your own back yard. My back yard was the Triumph Mine for twenty years. It became a battle ground, a forum, and a graveyard for a part of America that I thought a lot of. When I arrived there in fall of 1973, it was a junkyard of ramshackle shacks and black dirt. There were forty cars shot full of holes up North Star Gulch and numerous other cars, trucks, and parts of steel machines scattered up and down East Fork. I krew nothing of the Triumph Mine. I grew up in Jersey, and came to Idaho to ski…

Within fifteen years from the end of World War II, the mining town of Triumph was beginning to look a little shabby. Many of the houses were empty. The big stamp mill had a fire in 1945, and the remains stood on the hillside as a monument to the old days. The new mill that was funded in 1946 did not get built until 1950. The money came from the NRA/Strategic Metals Program. What was strange with this new, cutting-edge *sink-float* mill was they decided not to retrieve the gold from the ore. They were having a hard time with the pyrite, and decided to wait for development of new electric processes that would make it more cost effective.

From 1889 to 1949, the Triumph Mining Company produced, on average, six one hundredths of an ounce per ton in gold, steady, like clockwork. But for some reason, even though President Roosevelt called in all the privately held gold in the nation, they left gold out of the new sink float mills flow diagram, and let it pass into the tailings for another day.

The new mill produced concentrate from 300 tons of ore per day. As the workings got further and further into the mountain, the cost to get the ore to the crusher increased; all the time, prices were falling. Gold prices had been artificially propped up by the National Recovery Administration in the 40s, but fell in the 50s. The new mill's Master Mill Man kept a daily record of the tail end of the mill line, or *the tailings*. When the crews in the mountain were having a hard time feeding the new crusher, the company began to rework the old tails and dumps. These contained high amounts of silver and gold because the old mill was inefficient.

But for the new mill, the party was over, and it was over for Averell Harriman, too, (the developer and benefactor of Sun Valley). Harriman went onto the world stage and ran for President against Ike, then settled for Governor of New York.

Baldy, the mountain, was bought by Bill Jans and he would reinvent Sun Valley over the next ten years.

The old mine foreman, Rupert, was still up East Fork. He owned most of it and was running some cows, raising his family in a shack-like home built out of lumber that he salvaged from buildings left on the mountain, his mountain. It was said that if you wanted to talk to Rupe, bring your hammer; his wife Bonnie would feed ya, but he would work ya.

Just another day at the Triumph Mineral Co.

The blue Ford pickup pulled up to the North Star Portal shed as Rupert noticed the door was open and the padlock was broken off again. *God damn it*, he thought, as he stepped into his building and looked over his gear. "These damn kids."

His son Bill quickly noticed the toolbox ajar and grease rags on the workbench. "These weren't kids, dad," he said and he pointed to the motor on the big yellow blower at the entrance to the tunnel. "They took our starter motor, Pop," said Bill. "I guess we ain't working today"

The blower pushes clean air down a fabric tube about twelve inches around for almost a halfmile into the workings. The new tunnel that Rupe was driving was headed toward the Minerva and Mary Claims. These claims were producing good ore, very good ore, when the Union workers demanded more money in the winter of 1958; the company bosses tried to explain to them that the company was barely making a profit because prices were almost half of what they were getting during the boom years of WWII. The union didn't care; they wanted more, always more, and they were linked with the strikes up in the Idaho panhandle that had become very violent at times.

In 1944, lead was seventeen cents per pound. In 1954, it was eleven. Workers in the mine were some of the highest paid around the state, but the unions still wanted more.

That's not to say it wasn't hard work. It was back-breaking work, and by 1970 Rupert's back looked like the coast highway, yet he still kept digging in the ground. "Every day is a new challenge in the mine," he once told me. "You can tell where you're going by understanding where you've been."

There was a blower at the mouth of the North Star tunnel with a 4-cylinder, air-cooled Wisconsin Engine. These engines were common on many machines, from pumps to welders. The missing starter was going to cost a few bucks, but more costly was the down time for the two sole employees of the Triumph Mineral Company.

Rupert had made a deal with the big bosses at the Federal Mining Co. in San Francisco to lease the mine for a token amount with a right to buy it. They never expected to mine it again. From their point of view, it was played out. Not because there wasn't ore, but because nobody needed it. The US military was the main buyer of strategic metals, and the flying stock of the USAF had switched to jets. Because jet fuel has no lead in it, lead prices fell.

Silver was holding its own and the Minerva Claim had shown almost sixty ounces per ton in some of its assays. That's real high and enough to make a man want to dig for it.

Rupert and his three sons Tony, Bill, and Pat, had constructed a 20 x 40 foot shed with a workbench and a large Atlas Copco diesel compressor. Hoses ran from the compressor into the portal of the North Star Tunnel, to a 200 gallon air storage tank and an air powered Mucking machine. This machine had a bucket on the front of it that lifted up over its head and dumped into an ore car pulled behind it. The rusty old machine was purchased new in 1938 by the company back in the glory days, and it still worked if you tinkered with it. Not today, not without fresh air. Men need fresh air to work in the mines. So they nailed the shed door shut, loaded in the truck and headed to the parts house in Hailey to order a new starter motor.

My crazy friend.

Milton sat in his reclining chair, his hands gripped on the ends of the arm rests. He was doing his morning affirmations. "Nothing but good shall come to me, nothing but good shall go from me."

He repeated this chant for about half an hour until his voice got louder and he was in a trance-like state, his head rocking in a circular motion, the well-worn leather chair creaking on its rocker springs.

Milton was a church man, a Lutheran from the Dakotas... He left his church when he had a vision to start a new church with a small band of followers. They believed that Jesus was from space. That's the easiest way to put it. It shocks most people, but they keep their mouths shut and just back away.

He and his wife, Vernet, lived in a little house on Main Street in Triumph. They had a daugther. They were very nice, honest, tidy, and simple people. The house was always perfect.

Milton owned a dozen old travel trailers that he pieced together and rented for very reasonable fees to young people who had moved up from all over.

He and his group bought the whole town of Triumph from the Company in 1965 or '66 for about sixty grand. In the deed, the Triumph Mining Company retained the rights to the roads, ditches, power and pump lines, as well as all the mineral rights and rights to the tailings thereon.

The tailings have about 30,000 ounces of gold in them, sitting quietly, along with lots of silver, lead and zinc, as well as cadmium, copper, and graphite.

The New Agers had a charter for a nonprofit philanthropic corporation that was dedicated to new age ideas. They called the town corporation Triumph Inc.

In the beginning, followers of Milton all took homes in the town. They used the old hotel as a community center, and would hold meetings and seminars there. The New Agers would come up from all over to talk about the great changes that were soon to take place on the planet. It was the Age of Aquarius, and the stars were lining up. The skies would surely open and the new age would begin.

Vernet communicated directly with planetary spirits. She would sit at her table with a white notepad and a pencil. As she began to chant up the spirits that were out in space, the wiry ole gal would transcribe the message onto the pad. *"There will be a great uprising of the violet transmuting flames, all the old will pass away and there will be new light."* And on and on for pages like this. Crazy? Who's to say? People can believe what they want in this country, as long as they don't hurt anybody.

She and Milton followed the Good Book, but they went beyond that. They had another book that described characters out in space, a kind of alter world of spirits that were looking over all of us, ready to step in to stop us from ruining the planet with war and pollution. That sounded okay to me. I'm a Catholic and we pray to saints. We got a saint for everything. So space, why not?

Milton was a character. He had a real weird sense of humor. He loved to twist Bible stories into life lessons: "You got to separate the wheat from the chaff," he would say.

His brother, Ernie, was a different kettle of fish. Ernie was more of an entrepreneur and he set out to build the 8th Wonder of the World. *The Great Wooden Hill.* This would be a go-cart track, with a large wooden ramp over the building that now sits on East Fork Lane in Triumph.

APRIL 1969

This insane mix of new religion, utopian ideas, and the remnants of an industrial complex the war effort left behind sat quietly up the East Fork of the Wood River.

Milton was a dedicated churchman. He was an ordained Lutheran, but he followed the teachings of a guy named Emanuel Swedenborg.

Now this guy Swedenborg lived in the mid-1700s, right smack in the heart of the Reformation, at a place called *The Great Copper Mountain*. His father owned a big chunk of the copper mine and was filthy rich. The Great Copper Mountain wasn't really a mountain, as much as a pit that produced 70% of the world's copper beginning in the 5th century and officially closing in 1994.

From 500AD to the 1800s, copper, lead, zinc and gold were produced by first building a fire on the surface and letting it burn all night, then come morning, the rock would be cracked and cooked, thus making it easier to remove. Ancient Romans quenched the fires with streams of water, another method of using thermal stress to free the ore.

All of the great domes of Europe and Britain were clad with copper from Sweden. The mine would have hundreds of fires every night, smoking up the air of the village of Falun. Drunkenness and madness were common among the miners, and so was scientific research. The chemist, Jon Jacob Berzelius, built a laboratory at Falun. JJ was the guy that first laid out the Periodic Chart. This was a time when church and science were clashing daily. It was stylish to hate all things Vatican and like any good repressive regime, the Vatican denounced them all as heretics. Nothing ever really changes.

Emanuel was a pretty smart kid and wrote a bunch of stuff about mineralogy. Hanging out in this world of boiling beakers and chemical distillery, my guess is he started *tripping the light fantastic* because he began writing profusely about life after death, life on other planets, and connections between married couples after death.

Early mineralogy received a lot of flak from the Church in Rome. Alchemists were labeled occultists and science was evil. Many alchemists were consumed with two ideas. Idea number one was the creation of an elixir that would extend life. They cooked, boiled, mixed, and after a few hundred years, came up with whiskey. That wasn't quite what they were searching for, but a pretty good discovery anyway. The other thing alchemists were obsessed with was turning lead to gold. Boiling lead and adding stuff will probably make you crazy, always has, always will, and if you follow Alice into Wonderland, anything can happen.

Emanuel spent the first half of his life as an alchemist, nose over a test beaker screwing around with lead and trying to crack the secret code that would make him richer. Instead he began to hear voices, directly from space gods.

Swedenborg wrote two really big volumes called *The Heavenly Doctrine* and *The Heavenly Mysteries*. In these thick books, he would go on and on about how there are other planets, other worlds more advanced than ours that watch over us, and keep us from screwing up. Jesus was from one of those places and he came here on a flying machine.

Swedenborg even drew plans for this machine as it was revealed to him, and guess what? It looked like a flying saucer.

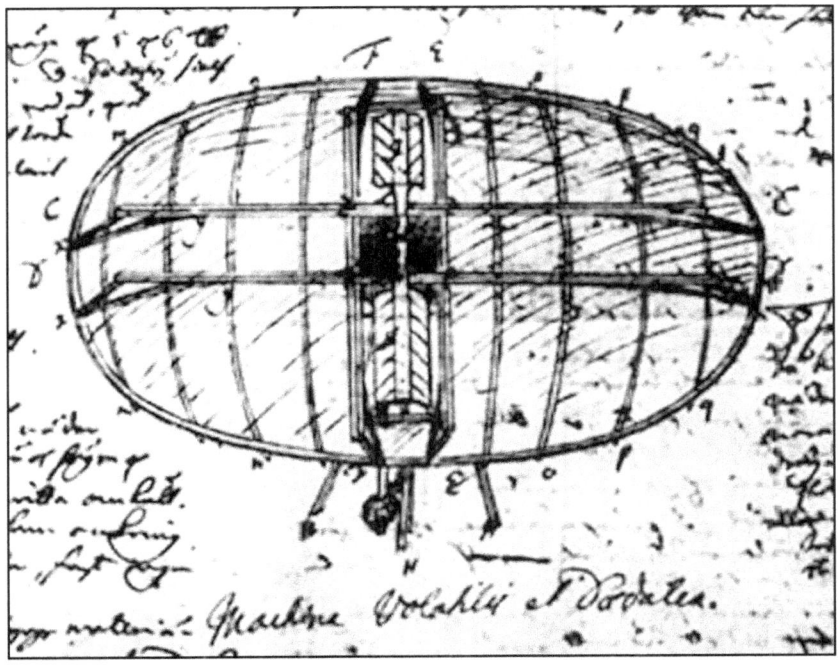

In these volumes, there were other characters too, Sanada, Vishnu, and others. I don't know, a shit load of spaceguy super saints. People in the northern European countries and England ate this stuff up. It combined the best of all the paganism from the Norse and Scots. It dealt with divorce, it trampled Rome into the ground, and everybody liked that in northern Europe in the 1700s.

This guy Swedenborg set the foundation for all the New Age religions that sprouted during the Age of Aquarius. Some theologians claim Joseph P. Smith incorporated some of Swedenborgism into the creation of the Book of Mormon.

But back in Triumph, Milton and Vernet not only followed, but communicated directly with these space gods. It's a free country, I say, go for it if it floats your boat. Just don't park in my space, I'm workin.'

Now I'm an openminded guy. Sure I lean to the right, but I'll take a look at almost anything. I read several pages of Swedenborg's *Heavenly Doctrine* and my head almost exploded. I can say, without a doubt, that this guy was a classic fruitcake.

Living in the limelight.

I was hired by the Sun Valley Ski School in the winter of 1973/'74. I had dropped out of Columbia School of Architecture after a year and a half. The Architecture school was in Orange County, New York, near Vernon Ski Area where I was on staff at the Ski School. Nobody wanted to go to the downtown campus in Harlem in 1971, are you kidding? New York was a dirty, crime infested hellhole.

When I got to Ketchum, I rented a little office in the Devil's Bedstead Building and was drawing log cabin plans and singing in the Crazy Horse Saloon. Ketchum was full of wild young people who had all escaped from somewhere, Berkeley, 'Nam, the East Coast; Ketchum was a non-stop, full-time party in 1974-'75. No rules, just right.

I showed up for Ski School lineup on the top of Baldy. It was post-Christmas week and the town was busy. Rhiner was the boss, and as he went down the line with daily assignments, he got to me.

"Carlo," he said.

"Yo," I responded.

"You are to report to Dollar Mountain immediately!" he barked with his thick Austrian accent. "You have a group private."

Really? I thought. That meant a few extra bucks. I headed down the hill, jumped into my Blazer and hurried over to Sun Valley's beginner area, Dollar Mountain. I put on my gear and reported to the supervisor. I used my father's name, Carlo, when I got here because there were several Karls on the ski school. I thought it would help me stand out some. I took ski instructing pretty seriously back then. I liked it, and threw myself into the fray with vigor.

So here I was in the base area. Three people were off to the side waiting for me. I introduced myself to these folks and helped them get their gear on. The group was composed of a young, stocky boy of 14 or 15 named Miko, a small, wiry woman named Helena, and a stocky man about my height, who wore a full face mask and did not tell me his name.

The day went pretty normally. I figured the mask guy must have burns or something, because it was a sunny day and pretty warm. The woman was very strong and she picked up the moves really fast. She was very coordinated, and was skiing within a few hours. The kid did okay, but he liked to clown around. The masked man did well also, and by the end of the day, they had conquered Dollar Mountain.

Helena had a kind of special energy. I don't know how to put it, exactly, chutzpa, confidence, she was very likeable, and so was the kid. The man was very quiet and just tailed along. But I guess they liked it well enough, as they wanted to do the same the next day. That was fine by me, I needed the extra money.

At the end of day two, Helena said, "We would like to have you over for drinks at our house later."

She gave me the address and I found myself ringing the bell on a giant home on the Sun Valley Golf course at 4:00.

"Come in…" said Helena, "What are you drinking?"

"Johnny Walker Red," I said. "Rocks." I walked down a few steps into a great room with a terrific view and on the other side of the room, sitting in a window seat, was the guy with the face mask, Marlon Brando. It was like a candid camera moment and he knew it. *Very cool*, I thought. The house belonged to Francis Ford Coppola. The Italian thing, that's why Rhiner put me with these guys, it was a set up.

Thanks, Pop, I thought. My father told me skiing was a waste of time and I always tried to prove him wrong. The real story of *The Godfather* was first written about a woman, not a man. Mario Puzo changed it up for Hollywood and it was one of the all-time great movies.

Marlon was at the top of his game, and I was honored to get to know him. We became friends and at the end of the week, he sat me down and asked me a bunch of questions, like a quiz: "How would you survive if you were stuck in the winter wilderness?" he said.

I rattled off some bullshit, confident I could survive anywhere in winter. Winter was my friend, I was on the night shift ski patrol in high school and on the Ski School. Give me some dry gloves and a ski jacket and I'm good.

The next day Marlon wanted to go up Baldy. He was turning and stopping; they all were, especially Helena. I didn't realize she had just come off a movie called *Kansas City Bomber* where she beat the hell out of Raquel Welch on roller skates. Roller skates are just like skis. If you can skate, you can ski. I know this because I had taught the cast of the Broadway play *Applause Applause* with Lauren Bacall, a few years earlier at Vernon Valley in Jersey. The play was a musical on skates, and they took to skiing like ducks to water.

So I met my students at the house that morning about 9:00 AM Helena made me breakfast and we all got really friendly. They made me feel like family, so I put my two cents on the table.

"If you really want to go up Baldy," I said, "You need a ski outfit."

They had all showed up in jeans with long johns, leather work gloves, etc. They looked like crap, but more importantly, they were also freezing.

"Let's go shopping," said Marlon. "You can be our procurer." He smiled that Godfather smile and we loaded up in the rented Suburban. "You drive," he said, and he tossed me the keys.

We hit Pete Lane's ski shop like a whirlwind. When a truck full of Hollywood stars hit the ski shop with their instructor, the sales staff hops. Good gloves, real underwear, and Aumba one-piece ski suits for everyone.

They were all kind of blown away by how good they looked and how comfortable they were. The day before, they were wet and cold with fingers frozen; now they were dressed for winter.

Marlon was like "I can't believe how good this feels..." and he was stroking his arms and chest with his warm gloves.

Up the chair we went from River Run. I took them down College, then Olympic. They did great. They were warm and confident, so I took them over to Warms Springs, keeping to the cat tracks. Things were going fine until Marlon stopped on the cat track atop of Grey Hawk. He looked down at one of Baldy's steepest runs and said. "I want to go down that..."

"No way!" I said. "You're not ready for that. You'll break every bone in your body."

"I want to go down that. You take my skis. I want to slide down," he insisted.

There was about eight inches of new snow that morning. It was cold and clear, a perfect Sun Valley day, as Marlon Brando took of his skis and began to roll down Grey Hawk in his new, one piece jump suit, caressing the snow, laughing like a little kid, and doing what most skiers would find, to say the least, different.

I shadowed him with his skis and poles on my shoulder. When we got to the bottom of the steep part, we still had a quarter mile of flats to get to the base lodge and the soft snow was difficult to walk in. Marlon was clearly tired; Baldy had been a challenge for him.

"Let's get your skis back on," I said.

"No. I'll walk. You go on," he motioned.

I couldn't leave my private student and go on; that just isn't how things were done.

"Here. Stand on the back of my skis and hold onto me," I said. "Come on, sweetheart, hold me tight." I did my best Bogart.

So he carefully got on and we slowly proceeded down the very gentle bottom towards the Warm Springs Lodge.

Just my luck, Sepi, the Assistant Director of the Ski School, was in the chair going over us at that very moment and out came his little pocket notebook and pencil.

The next day, they called me into the office and I got chewed out Austrian style. "You represent the ski area. We gave you a very important celebrity. If he got hurt, it would bring bad publicity to the company..." Blah, blah, blah. They went on, quite excited, culminating in the unforgettable phrase: "You're fired."

My gravy train had jumped the track. I tried to explain to my boss, Rhiner, that you don't tell this guy what to do. Truth be told, they were looking for a reason to dump me. I was involved in a lawsuit on a construction project I had done during the summer. The woman who stiffed me and my crew had filed a counter claim, and it was in the papers. Thanks to a smart young attorney named Jim Philips, I won the case that spring and was able to pay my helpers, but that didn't help me at this moment.

I kept it to myself that evening when Marlon took me to dinner at the Warms Springs Ranch restaurant. The whole trip had been a whirlwind to me. I was in way over my head with these folks.

"I would like you to take my son, Miko, and take care of him," Marlon said, as the waitress poured the water glasses and took away the plates.

Now let me put things in perspective here. I was the Après-ski entertainment at the Crazy Horse Saloon on Tuesdays, Wednesdays, and Thursdays. For this I was paid forty bucks, tips, all the booze I needed and club sandwiches. Dave Cropper was the bartender. Jimmy, my best pal from Stowe, was the bar manager and Chris DuPont owned the joint. On Fridays, we had wet t-shirt contests. These were joyous occasions where we would all get tanked and pour warm soapy water on Ketchum's most beautiful and willing women.

Now I ask you, do I sound like the kind of guy you would want to take care of your teenage son?

Marlon's first son was into hard drugs in Los Angeles, and he didn't want that for Miko. So I guess, in hind sight, the Crazy Horse was almost like a health spa; just good old fashioned beer, burgers, and booty.

Marlon's office set me up in a condo out in Elkhorn, furnished, and I enrolled Miko in Wood River High.

I had absolutely no idea what I was getting myself into. I was just winging it as usual. I was shoveling roofs for Louie Stuir at Elkhorn and making plenty of money, lots more than Ski School. I even tried to bring Miko up on the roof with me, but that was a bad idea.

Miko was raised in Hollywood. I had no clue what that meant. I was trying to be a surrogate father, and instill some kind of work ethic or sense of thrift in the lad. What a fool I was. Miko was shackled to the Hollywood office. He had no cash, none, but he had a credit card that would be paid by the Brando Company. He was under a huge shadow—a giant Hollywood problem. He had a bigger-than-life dad to live up to, but also he was constantly being hit up for stuff, crazy stuff, like, one night he gets a call from a movie guy in Italy wanting to hire him to star in a movie. He was only 16, and girls would hit on him like crazy.

I began to see that this kid, who had the best attitude, always laughing and joking, had a real problem.

I tried to teach him to drive in an old '47 Ford pickup I had. I suggested it be his first truck, so he could get his first dings in on an old beater. I wasn't thinking Hollywood style.

Miko just went down to the Ford dealer and drove off in a brand new 4 x 4 with a roll bar, field lights and big tires. Black. The kid had style.

One night, I'm at the condo, and I get a call from Louie's Pizza. "Hello," I said.

"Mr. Massaro, this is Jane at Louie's in Ketchum, and I have a young man down here that is picking up a large tab on a credit card and we need authorization…"

"What kind of tab?" I said.

She explained that Miko had taken the entire Wood River High School football team and the cheerleaders to dinner.

"He can't do that," I said. "I don't want him buying his friends."

Well, that was a mistake. The kids had to call their parents to come down and bail them out. Miko was pissed at me and apparently so was *the office* when they found out.

He had developed a crush on a cute little thing named Cindy House, yep Rupert's daughter, and Miko had plans. Seems he would rather live in the same house with Cindy than me. I couldn't blame him, so he told his dad that I was out and Cindy was in.

Marlon flew up and had a powwow with Rup at the old homestead. Rupert was a shrewd, experienced horse trader, and managed to get fifteen hundred per month for room and board. I got the boot. This whole whirlwind was a lot for my over-inflated and now deflated ego. I had to recover, so I thought I would run a race.

There was a downhill coming up sponsored by United Airlines, with prize money, and I figured I would run it and make some dough and cling to the limelight a little longer. That didn't happen.

While pretending to be *The Down Hill Racer*, I was bumped ever so slightly by another skier. I got off course and ran into a solid, eight-inch sign pole on Mid River Run. I was broken. If I had hit my head, I would be dead or drooling. Instead, I broke my lower left arm (both bones), my kneecap, and took a chunk out of my hip bone that's a painful reminder that I would live with for years.

I had gone from the fast lane to a dirt road in a few short weeks. I had no home and no job. I was in the Sun Valley Hospital, laid up, so I made the call to my ole man back in Jersey.

My dad was really pissed at me for leaving him and going west. We had a father and son building business. I did the framing, and I left to gallivant around the west while he was left struggling through the recession of 1973. He had several spec houses that were not selling and he needed his son. I had left him.

"Dad…" I said. "I'm in the hospital. I broke my arm. I need you to send money."

"You want money, go to work," he said. "I'll tell your mother to say a rosary for you. You're a big boy. Good luck." And he hung up.

They cast me up and I made a deal to shovel the hospital roof, in my cast, to pay my bill.

Then Jimmy and I came up with a money maker of an idea: A spring concert in the Limelight Room of the Sun Valley Inn.

Help Stamp Out Cabin Fever was a huge success. We printed up flyers and bribed the maids with free tickets to put them under the pillows in the rooms. We put flyers on toilet doors. We gave the headliner slot to Archie Turner, an older, wiser fiddler champion.

Joe Cannon and I did a few numbers, then we all played together and the room loved it. We made about five grand that night. I paid the bands, paid my hospital bill, and bought a used Chevy 4 x 4. I had lost the new Blazer to the repo man when I broke my arm, so I had been gimping around town with a cane. I didn't see Miko much anymore. He settled in with Rupert's family on the East Fork Ranch.

What's out Eastfork?

I couldn't pay rent. I had my tools taken and my airless paint sprayer. I had to sell my welder. I was having a hard time making ends meet. Sometimes a simple, little machine can make the difference between eating and starving. Once I got the cast off, I was playing my guitar and that got me by, so I pursued that.

I began to play with a fine, young woman named Mia Carrol. She had talent, was on the ski school and was from the East Coast.

Mia was a good singer and played lots of the folksongs I did. We were good friends, and began to work together as a duo. We had no attraction towards each other that way; we were just buds, and began to travel around Idaho playing cowboy bars.

One day at her house in Hailey, I met a guy named Dan Tucker. Tucker had a '47 Chevy truck with a forge built into the back and was shoeing horses. We became friends, and he showed me how to shoe horses.

I had horses in South Jersey, but we just trimmed the hoofs because the sand didn't require shoes. It was hard work, tough on the back. I'd found a barn up East Fork that I was interested in, and Dan and I drove up to look at it. It was ten thousand dollars for the barn and a little house behind it. I tried to get the down payment together, but I couldn't. The owner, a little old woman named

Hulda Harr, Milton's sister, owned it and she would carry the paper for ten years at 10%. It think Dan was able to get the deposit from his parents, so he bought it.

Soon after, a young couple named Jim and Margaret Bradford pulled into town in a VW micro bus and lived on the loading dock on the west end of the barn. I moved into a loft room for a while, but Dan wanted his space. So I moved down to the river and set up a summer camp by the mouth of a cave. It was a good solid, hard rock tunnel that went back about 200 feet, to where the earth stayed 55 degrees no matter how cold it got outside. It was actually a pretty good camp for a young man. There was a swimming hole down there and plenty of good, dry pasture. In later years, the area would become Beaver Swamp, but back then it was dry land and beautiful.

Triumph began to fill up with young people who, one by one, replaced the New Age group. The religion of the new age is an open, less-structured doctrine. It sprang from the Reformation, a movement that by its very nature challenged the status quo. Divorce was strictly prohibited in the Roman Catholic doctrine and man might find himself with a *gumad*, a second woman, on the side. This would make him a sinner, and subject to the basket on Sunday.

Think about it; you could break the rules of the 15th century doctrine if you just showed up on Friday, made a confession to your local priest, and then put a few coins in the basket. What a racket. Then they would take the money and expand the franchise.

With the new age, a doctrine written in 1720, you could just divorce the wife, or have several soul mates that might lead to a tryst behind the milk barn. That's what happened to Milton's group. They switched wives and soon wanted out.

Melvin Swanson switched wives with Victor Atlinger and they were all okay with that for a while. Then the group wanted out, so they had to describe the parcels the little houses were on. Then they could whack things up and sell.

Brother Ernie had spent a lot of time building his Wooden Hill go-cart track on the tailings in the center of town. The first few test rides were a failure, as the dusty tailings quickly killed the motors of the go-carts. Ernie had an affair with a woman living in a little house on East Fork Lane, and had a heart attack in her bed. So they hired a surveyor from Twin Falls who was cheap and had the "Wooden Hill Plat" drawn up. They named the streets after themselves; then the turnover began.

The next generation, my generation, began to move in and Milton, Karst, Aldinger, and Swanson carried paper for a new group of truth seekers, looking for a small piece of America, out of the wind, next to a stove and a warming fire.

All that glitters...

The workings of the world financial system were rooted in a bimetal currency. That is to say, the king controls the coinage and can dilute the coinage as he deems necessary to run his kingdom. A ten dollar gold coin is presumed to be pure gold, but if the king has to fight the roving, Mongol hordes, he may need to stretch his funds—or borrow more funds from a money lender. The king might tell the Master of the Treasury to clip coins, add other cheaper metals to the coinage (tin usually, or copper), and spice up the face to look extra important—so the citizenry of the realm feel confident that, within their kingdom, their coins were golden. Then, in an effort to lighten the load, a paper note promising to be redeemable in silver or gold would be issued by a banker or money lender.

The Triumph Mine had sent tons of silver and gold to the treasury over the 85 years it operated, and Wall Street would leverage it up ten or twenty times in the financial instruments it peddled.

In the 1940s, President Roosevelt drove a nail in that coffin and bankers continued to push to make the bimetal myth a dinosaur. Paper was the future, backed by the full faith of the Government. Does that sound suspect? It does to me; it did to Dorothy, Toto, William Jennings Bryant, and the rest of the Silverites too.

Conspiracy theorists claimed Kennedy was planning on going back to the silver standard, and in fact he had printed new money that he was planning on circulating that would be redeemable in silver.

The bankers, the famed 4 horsemen, are all part of the Rothschild fiefdom in Europe, but I think Chase and Bank of America are like little horsemen, too; they are on ponies, riding behind.

Some people have said they killed Kennedy, others say it was the mob, some even say it was Frank Sinatra—because he was stood up on that big Florida trip. I think that story has legs because, for me, if I had cooked and cleaned, and planned for company, and then they canceled at the last minute and go up the street to somebody else's place, fuggetaboudit… I would be pissed too.

But regardless, silver was rumored to be ready to spike. That allowed Rupe to find some investors, and lease the mine with an option to buy it.

The first time I met Rupert, he was on the roof of the sawmill building, up on what we call the bench. The bench was a large cut about 200 feet above East Fork Road that held all the working buildings of the main portal of The Triumph. Rupe was up on the flat roof. The roofing was long gone and he was pulling off boards, saving every nail in a tin can; and his son Bill was passing the boards down, loading them onto a rickety trailer hooked onto the back of his pickup truck. The truck had a cattle cage on the back, obviously home-welded. It was made of used salvage pipe with horse shoes welded in for bracing.

"Hey…" I said. "This is a good building. Why are you tearing it down?"

"Who are you?" he snapped. "This is my building. I'll do what I want to with it."

He was not used to a stranger on his land questioning his actions.

"If you let me put a sawmill up here, I could cut you new lumber instead of this old junk." I had his attention. "You're cracking half of them pulling them off anyway..."

When I was just out of high school, I began to sell barn wood from old sheds and barns up in Sussex County, New Jersey. At one point, I was making two grand a week selling barn wood and beams to a broker in Manhattan. Every bar in New York was re-doing the interiors with old wood and beams. It was post Woodstock and we were all getting *back to the land that set our souls free...* And what better place to do that than a bar? I was very familiar with pulling and salvaging boards. If they crack, you can't get paid. "There was a sawmill up here..."

"How did you know that?" he said.

"Can't have a mine without a mill," I said.

As a kid I spent a lot of summers around the mines in north Jersey near Franklin and Hamburg collecting rocks. George Washington had built several water-powered forges up there, and left these big, stone pyramids with massive chimneys inside for making cannons and shot. Rocks and mining had always fascinated me, and my mother would tag along carrying the rocks.

"Come down to the house tonight for dinner and we will talk about it," he said. "It's the ranch down there," he pointed down the valley. From the bench, the whole valley spread out. It was all open as far as you could see, with a lot of hayfields. Rupert's ranch was composed of three parcels, totaling about 1,000 acres.

As foreman of the Triumph for many years, he was a big earner in the county. He had acquired land that really could not support itself without another income to the household. The East Fork of the Wood River is a beautiful basin, but it is the high desert and it can be harsh. Some years there will be no rain, others will see 30 inches of snow at the end of April. It can stay 20 or 30 below zero for weeks. I have seen seven inches of rain fall overnight up at the Mascot Mine, taking rocks the size of a truck down the creek and snapping Douglas-fir trees forty inches around like toothpicks; but most things move in "geology time." You got to be there a lifetime to see it.

Photo: Pat House

Hello, come in, sit down ...

As you entered Rupert's home, you felt as though you were passing into a time warp. Everything, every board, hinge, railing, and window, had already lived a full life somewhere else. Today, with all this Green certification crap, he would get a platinum rating, because everything was recycled. EVERYTHING.

He made lots of little windmills that would spin like crazy in the afternoon as the sun drove the air up the valley. There was a wood shed with a large circular cutoff saw that ran off a flat belt-driven tractor PTO, and a small Ford tractor. Rupert liked Fords. He always bought a Ford. In the corner of the yard was a new, shiny, black Ford 4x4 that I recognized as Miko's.

As I was coming in, he was headed out.

"Gotta go..." he said. "Good to see you."

"How are you?" I said.

"Fine, great. I'm off to the school. There's a basketball game tonight." And with that he was gone.

I entered the house and the wood stove was warm. Bonnie sat me down at the kitchen table, poured me some coffee, and set out a dish of Oreo cookies.

Rupert was coming up from the barn. I couldn't help notice that this guy never stood still. He was feeding cows, cutting firewood, digging in the mountain, tearing down buildings. He had a lot of go, all the time. He reminded me of my dad; he was the same way, always doing something, every minute. I guess that might be a secret to success and happiness, forward motion.

"So where did you grow up?" Bonnie started my interview. "He'll be up in a moment. He's just feeding the cows," she said.

As he passed the woodshed, he grabbed an arm full of wood and headed in. Rupe put the wood in a box near the stove, hung his coat on a hook at the door, and came into the kitchen.

He was now in his office. Behind him, at the table, was a tall, five-drawer file cabinet. Bonnie placed a cup of coffee in front of him almost as soon as his butt hit the chair.

"What time is the Grange Dinner?" he said, letting me know very politely that I couldn't hang around long.

"Six," said Bonnie, confirming my assumption.

"Look…" I said, "I bought the old mill site from Milton Harr. Do you know Milton?" I asked.

"Oh, yes," said Bonnie, tinkering around in her kitchen. "They're a little different," she added.

"You ever see any flying saucers?" Rupe could be kinda loud sometimes.

"No," I said, moving on. "So I put a sawmill on the ore mill site."

Although the county Zoning Department said I could, they now have changed their mind and they want it out. I had lost everything again by that decision, and found myself so destitute that I applied for food stamps. I used them one time and felt so degraded that I began to go behind the grocery stores on Sundays and look for food in the dumpster.

"Damn dingbats…" he grabbed a cookie and dipped it in his coffee. "Have one…" he said.

I took another off the plate and Bonnie shook a few more from the paper tube in the Nabisco box.

"They said that I can't put a sawmill on an ore mill site. I can only put an ore mill."

"God damn dingbats…" he barked.

I had hit a nerve. This was good

"They just don't know nothing about…" he was getting louder. Bonnie came over to the table, took his coffee cup and patted him on his shoulder.

"Rupert…" she said, "We have to get ready for the Grange." She turned down the dial.

"How you gonna get power?" he asked. He was down to basics already, like he had made his decision and now he wanted production schedules.

"I'll get the power hooked up," I said.

"It's three-phase, you know." He stood up. "We had a lot of power when the mine was running."

"What will you charge me?" I asked.

"What can you pay?" he said, looking right through me.

"I don't have much money and I will have to make improvements to your building." I was horse trading with a pro, but holding my own and I think he liked that. "I'll give you one hundred dollars per year and one truckload of mill ends per year for the use of the shop for ten years.

I'll give you 20% of the scrap metal revenue, and twenty-five cents per yard on the waste rock and topsoil."

He didn't expect such a well thought out response. I come from an East Coast bunch of dagos that made their money taking things that nobody else wanted. Some people stereotype them, but I can tell you, waste management is a hard business, and just like Rupe, you can never sit still. Somebody is always making a mess somewhere that they don't want to clean up.

The Triumph Mine was a mess when I got there in '73. There were junk cars everywhere, shot full of holes; there were half-demolished buildings; giant pieces of twisted rusted iron… I'm talking hundreds of tons and close to a hundred cars; there was one inch cable—over a mile long, copper wire, three inches round that ran into the tunnels. The mountain stretched all the way to Elkhorn in Sun Valley, and there were more workings over there with more steel piled up, overgrown with aspen trees. It was a beautiful mess.

"Can I get a contract?" I was now feeling a little bold. 'I'm not the maid' was one of my mother's favorite phrases, and I was going to clean up someone else's mess.

"Write it up," he said, "but keep it simple, so we can understand it."

He ended our first meeting and then I went up to the camp. That's how Rupe and Bonnie referred to the Village of Triumph: *the camp*. Most families camped in tents. I was camping at the mouth of a cave, but as soon as I was emboldened with a contract, I felt like I could build something with it.

I shipped my first load of scrap iron to a small smelter in Provo, Utah that made steel tubing. It was about 20 tons and netted me about eight hundred dollars. The load was ten of the giant ore cars. I kept two. The rest went to the cooker; that's green.

I paid Rupe his share, and Bonnie fed me. This was a pattern that would continue for fifteen years. I would pay my royalty around diner time, mooch a meal, and hear what was happening in the courthouse.

Rupert went from head of the Hailey Garage, to the Commission, then two terms as County Commissioner. During those years, I had friends in the courthouse. Any friend of Rupe's was a friend of mine.

The county was growing in leaps and bounds. Giant homes were being built, homes that would keep twenty or thirty men working for a year or two. *Don't Californicate Idaho* was a cry heard commonly, yet people kept coming, and they had big bucks, so people kept building.

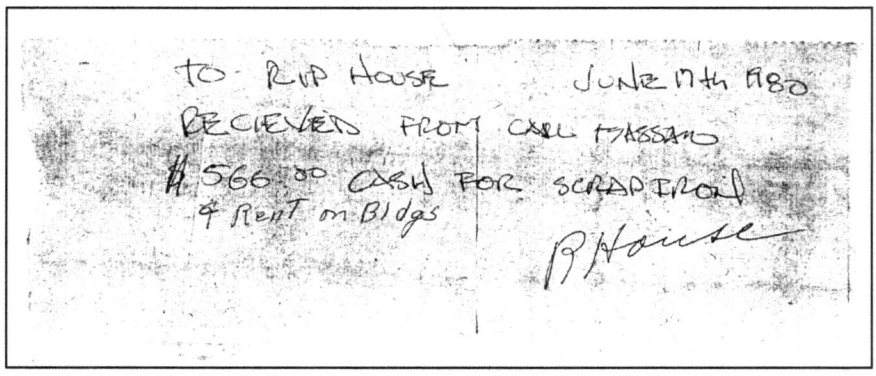

Call it all in.

In 1934, Roosevelt froze all gold sales and called in all privately owned gold. At the time, gold was selling for twenty-two bucks an ounce. The Feds took it all in and set a new price on the gold they held of thirty-five bucks. Thus, overnight, they made something from nothing, applauding their brilliance by announcing that the Great Depression would soon be over and there would be a chicken in every pot. Bullshit.

The Depression continued. Think about this for just a minute. You have some gold in your home, probably in the form of jewelry, maybe a coin or two, or maybe you're a small town bank with some bars in the vault. Uncle Sam declares by law you must turn them in for twenty-two dollars an ounce, payable in freshly printed paper currency. If you didn't comply, you could go to prison. Then after they tallied it all up, cooked it down, poured it into new bars with a stamp on it, they valued it at thirty-five dollars an ounce. It didn't work. It just made people poorer, and the government more powerful. Thus began the rise in our national debt.

You see, you can have all the philosophical rants about money, greed and power, but long before King Solomon, gold and silver were held as the symbol of legal tender.

Now the bimetal standard has been abused, misused, and confused by all kinds of swindlers and nations. But compared to the corruptive power of paper, gold is, well, golden.

In the middle of the village of Triumph there is a pile of tailings from the original North Star Mill. This mill was a stamp mill; that is to say, the ore was *stamped* by iron hammers driven by a camshaft, then the ore went to shaker tables and they vibrated the material that fell, or was fed onto the tables. The tables were about 70% efficient, maybe 80%. So 25% of the minerals that were removed by drilling and blasting, timbering, sawing, and grubbing in the deep dark earth are sitting in the crushed sand in these tailings piles. But, and this is a big but, there are about 1.4 lbs of lead per ton and our EPA now says that raw lead is as dangerous as Tetra Ethal Lead (TEL). That's a policy change that shut down most mines in the Rockies and moved ore production to South America, Canada, China, Australia — anywhere but here.

Now, the new people would laugh at the thought of processing this material. I have been chastised numerous times by Vernet, who thought there was no need for material wealth because she was sure that the New Age was coming soon and we wouldn't use money, we would all communicate by telepathy.

Turns out, Vernet could see the future and it was the freedom card — where people don't need money, they don't have to work; they just use this card, swipe it and magically a transfer is made.

One day she came up to my house and really got into it with me. "All you want is the gold," she said, "that's all you care about. Come on, Milton..."

He just smiled at me and dutifully followed her down the road. She didn't correlate with poor Milton's duties that required him crawling around under the rickety old trailers he scabbed together, that were always freezing up in winter—and the dozen single moms who lived in there, forking over the rent to Milton, who in turn, forked it over to Vernet. The aliens in her schizophrenic noodle didn't send her cash. Her daily bread was coming from the lands that Milton was carrying paper on, lands that were purchased by a nonprofit, religious corporation dedicated to philanthropic and religious works.

Ah, the life of a junk man.

After I loaded up 40,000 pounds of scrap iron that was scattered all over the mine property, the truck rolled down East Fork Road and headed to the steel mill in Provo.

They sent me another check for eight hundred bucks and change, and I had it converted into silver dollars. I had begun to hoard coins in ammo boxes. I had them buried in the back of the cave under some rock. Silver dollars make a nice impression. I put two hundred on Rupe's kitchen table for his share of the scrap, as per our agreement, and seven hundred on Milton's table as a payment on the mill site footings known as *Block 7* in the Wooden Hill Sub.

The mill site was covered with lead ore, black rock, and more steel and debris. People don't realize what a mess Triumph was when we all arrived in the early seventies.

Now, many local folks love to complain about the heartless industries that lay waste to the land and wreak havoc on the planet. But the company had one client and only one: The Department of Interior.

Under contract, they told the company what to pay, supported by the unions, how much to produce, and they set the price by the NRA (National Recovery Act). The price was actually increased by a bunch, inflated by stimulus programs designed to get men working. That did work, but when the carcass was picked clean, there was no money held back to clean up or reclaim the site. It was like the party suddenly stopped and the dance hall was left empty with cigarettes and empty bottles scattered around.

Rupert built his whole ranch from the salvage of the mine buildings, and I, too, started my life with the same. We grow strong on what our enemies leave behind.

Time to settle down.

The Ketchum Police Department had been getting calls about the goings on at the Crazy Horse Saloon. It was a *den of sin*. The owner, Chris DuPont, took the advice of his fiancé and decided to dump it, so he leased it to some guys who were going to change it up. *The News Stand* was the new name. It was going to have lots of old style pinball machines, a selection of all the major city newspapers, and fine cigars.

George Liabe was a character with a great attitude. He was a show business guy with lots of national county fair booking contacts. If custom would merit a top hat and cane, George would have worn one.

He hired me to build a rough sawn wainscot and rough sawn tables. My sawmill was working, and I got busy. I had purchased my land from Milton: four acres for seven thousand dollars; 10% down; 10 years at 10% interest, and was making a payment each month. The payment would usually involve a visit and a sermon from Milton about his beliefs.

Between Milton's and Vernet's lectures on new age alien mumbo jumbo, Rupert's can-do, old school commonsense, and my Roman Catholic upbringing, I stand before you as one totally fucked-up individual. But having walked around the base of the mountain, and getting a good idea of what comes from inside the mountain, I was ready to begin climbing the mountain.

We all have to dance at the Ball sometime. I had fallen in love with a woman named April Houg. She was Norwegian, blond, blue/green eyes, very pretty and very strong. She was willing to come live with me down by the river. We decided to play house in an old, abandoned log cabin near my cave camp.

We swept it out. I fashioned a heavy door with a chainsaw and my horseshoe rasp. We put plastic sheeting over the windows, and I whipped up a steel woodstove out of a large transformer cover. I was a hobo with a hot girlfriend; a hippie. Holy shit, how did this happen? Well it did, and I was crazy about her. We created a life.

I bought a military surplus GMC 6 x 6 deuce and a half that was in really good condition, like new almost, from a guy in Hagerman who carried the paper. Interesting how simple life is without banks. People just are forced to make a deal, and most of the time they work out.

Once I got this truck, I called my old man: "Pop," I said, "Can you come out here? I have an arrangement with the miner here that I think is worth looking at."

My pop was a Bosun in the US Navy, North Africa, Anzio beach, and then the march through Italy. We always had boats. We were raised on the water; everything was kept ship shape on our dock. The ropes were coiled, the decks were scrubbed and varnished, every year like clockwork. I was going to get a review of my shanty, truck, and sawmill. It all needed to be squared away tight. He said he would come in the fall after Labor Day, so I had the summer to pull my shit together.

I decided to build a little house on a 20 x 20 foundation that was left on my mill site. It was what was left of a garage built by Jack Rutter. I began one afternoon in earnest; I had lumber, logs and a pile of used, rusty 20 penny nails that I found in the mine. I started with a post and lintel system, copying the notching that Jack Rutter used on the ore shoots.

The building would be one square room with a ship ladder in the center servicing a bedroom upstairs. I had a 1930s vintage, Sears potbelly stove that would supply the heat. I had no money, as in *none*. I had a chain saw, sawmill, and hand tools. I got the walls up in a few days; Milton came by and watched.

"You need water," he said.

Now across the street from my land was the firest house in Triumph. It was built for the foreman of the Triumph Mine, but now belonged to Donald Ramsey. Donnie owned the Chevy dealership in Ketchum on Main Street. He was worried shitless that I had pulled in a diesel powered sawmill and was building a shack across from his fine, red brick house.

His best bud, Bob Barns, was Blaine County's very first Building Inspector. They had just started with codes in the early seventies and the law was new. So one day I'm out in the clear Idaho air on my land, with Milton hanging out. We were talking about his new age stuff, laughing and enjoying the day—when ole Bob pulls up and says I got to stop work because I was violating the new law. He made the mistake of first pulling up to Donald's house and checking in.

Now, my dad was a builder, as were my cousins, my uncles, my grandfather and his grandfather, back to some poor mope slapping flat bricks into a Roman wall. So corruption by inspectors is nothing new, but Milton's approach to this problem was just a tad different.

Bob pulls up (by the way, I hold no grudge against Bob or Donnie, as time went on, Donald was one of the best neighbors I ever had) in a big Jeep Wagoneer Woodie.

He's got his cowboy hat and his rodeo buckle, and he rolls down the window.

"Howdy..." He's got this grin, like a rattler just before a strike.

Milton is standing in the road and I'm within the four partially-framed walls of my little house to be.

"Who's building this?" He asked.

Before I could respond, Milton took charge: "Men from space," Milton asserted with a strong North Dakota accent.

See, the main metaphor in all off Milton's doctrine is that we are, in fact, standing in space, on the surface of a big blue ball, sailing through the universe with a bazillion other planets. Thinking about it that way, he was telling his truth as he viewed it. But Bob was not really prepared for that. Nothing throws people off more than a rattle to their doctrine.

"Men from space, eh?" said Bob, his eyes locked on this crazy man whom he had never met, but had heard rumors about, I'm sure.

"Yes," said Milton. His voice was very loud, like on a pulpit, preaching to his flock. "They come in the night and work with lamps..." and with that Milton took a step closer to Bob, and he was visibly shocked, like Milt might put the hexo on him. "This is a church," said Milton.

Bob was disarmed; with that he put the car in reverse and backed down to Donald's house. There it stood for a while, and then he left.

"Hello," from Area 51.

One late summer day, I was cutting boards on my sawmill when a man approached. I shut down the machine, and as the old wheels coasted to a stop:

"Hello," he said, with the same kind of Dakota accent as Milton. "I'm Colonel Wayne Aho." He was very self-confident. "I'm from the New Age Foundation."

Oh shit, I thought, *Jehovah's Witness.*

He went on to explain that he was a big mucky muck in the Air Force and was somehow associated with the infamous Project Blue Book from Area 51, flying saucer central, and he went on…

"…Spirit has revealed to me that we will have a new age soon," he said.

I looked around; it was a normal day. I had fuel, a peanut butter sandwich; bring it on, I thought.

At this point my little house was framed up. He asked if I would like to stay in his New Age headquarters and take care of it. I wasn't sure I was prepared to usher in the New Age at this point. I was halfway into cutting a thousand board feet of 1x6's and with my old mill… That would take a while.

We walked into a tin building right next to my little house that I never paid much attention to. It was full of flies; dead flies everywhere. It had been empty for many years and was full of books, strange books, New Age books, on all kinds of stuff: food, gardening, religion, alternative universes, how to build a space ship, on and on in hundreds of books. He asked me if I could pay rent—and I responded that I had a house, pointing to my little shack with no water, toilet or power—and said I would be doing him a service taking care of the place. It was a mess, but really just needed a good scrub.

At first, April didn't want to move into it. She thought it was creepy, and some nights it was. The building was the mine office. It was built by Jack Rutter in 1937 and had a huge Mosler safe in the front room that was state of the art in 1890. Jack had moved it from a bank in Picabo and reinstalled it in a cement vault, then built the house around it. It was very cold, all the time, and hard to get warm in that house.

The building had huge electric heaters that cost a fortune to run. When the sun was out in the dead of winter, the house was warm and welcoming. But when the sun went down, the place was colder than my cabin down by the river. We had no woodstove, just the electric, and we couldn't afford to turn it on because the bill would be over a hundred and fifty bucks. For us, that was half of our income.

We lived in the front two rooms. I rigged up a kitchen sink in what was once a front office. Our bedroom was freezing, but we were young and that wasn't a problem. I got an old water heater and plumbed that into the bathroom, so we had hot water and a shower. That was uptown.

April and I became the caretakers of the *New Age Headquarters.*

By this time, the Village of Triumph had a pretty good group of folks, all young, with the exception of Milton and Don Ramsey. We did everything together. We had no TV; we had Thanksgiving in the Community Center that was the hotel. Wendy Collins organized ladies dances and exercise classes. April wrote little articles on herbs and wild plants, conducted field walks, seminars… We all had horses and would ride. We played music all the time. Triumph was a kind of free-spirited paradise for children of the seventies.

But we all smoked pot, lots of it and there were some folks that took other drugs too. Lucky for me, I was too poor to use coke or mushrooms. I was a cheap weed guy and I thought I was keeping it hidden from Milton and Rupert, but I wasn't. I was the fool on the hill. At first I would supplement my gallon jug of Gallo Burgundy with a toke around the campfire; we all did. But reefer is a hideous drug. Anybody who says it's safe is just not there yet. Eventually, it gets you, and you're addicted. I smoked a pipe full of tobacco too, so I was smoking something all the time. It's been over thirty years now since I quit and wouldn't go back ever. I can't even stand the smell.

Bill and Wendy Collins became our best friends. Bill was very different from me; we came from different backgrounds. I grew up studying classical art and building. I started very young, like eight, doing study copies of Leonardo's sketches. My father went to a special art school in Newark called Arts High, and was very good at oils. We, both my brother and I, were taught to paint. We were all encouraged to read and study. My dad never watched TV. He sat in the kitchen with a book.

I think Bill grew up in rural Alabama and the schools there were different than the schools in North Jersey. But Bill was a good father, and worked hard building condos and town houses.

I had left New Jersey after working on garden apartments and huge housing projects in the wetlands of Long Beach Island. We had to frame a house every four days. I swore I would never work for a developer doing tract projects again. And for the most part, I steered clear of ski town condos unless I was really hungry. I could make enough playing my guitar to feed myself, and I had the big truck and the mill.

That fall, my Pop came out and gave me five grand to buy a well-used 955 Caterpillar crawler loader. I could now move very heavy things and put them on my truck. I built a trailer out of an old 6 x 6 truck frame. I built a gravel plant from scratch; I was now working sixteen hours a day. I put a plow on my truck, then I got another truck; a 5-ton diesel, like new.

Within a few short years, I had a business up on the bench in the old mine shop and was grossing fifty grand. Not bad for a starving hobo.

One night I went down to pay my bill to Rupert, and as Bonnie was serving me up a plate of her home cooking, Rupe showed me a letter from the Getty Mining Company in California. Getty entered into a five-year exploration lease with the option to purchase from the Triumph Mineral Company, at fifty grand a year.

At first I was concerned about my agreement, and thought I would find myself out in the cold. My whole life evolved from the topsoil and gravel lease now.

Then Rupe explained that they would hire me to build the roads and be their subcontractor. I could lease a brand new dozer for the summer and make 65 bucks per hour.

In 1980, that was good money. Knowing that Getty was coming was a huge deal to me. Everyone else in Triumph worked in the trades on the big Sun Valley projects. They were slowly evolving into almost a guild; promoting each other and keeping their little cliques recommended. A clique I was out of, probably due to my outspoken dislike for the building racket and the code rules. I took another road, I would rather load rocks in the hot sun than work for some rich trophy wife on her dream kitchen.

I knew Getty would need a field office, so I approached Hulda Harr about buying the Pipefitters Building. We settled on a price of seventeen thousand dollars and I cleaned it out.

Hulda was a New Ager too, and the place was full of glass jars. I backed the dump truck up to the loading dock and just started throwing in jars. I rented the building to Getty for five years at five hundred per month, and my payment to Hulda was about one-fifty. This was my first rental, and it paid off the building.

Then one day, I bought the New Age Building in a transaction that deserves a detailed description...

"The Healing Hands."

In the late 1850s, some German dude theorized that, depending on when you are born, you are bound to be deficient in two or three of the twelve mineral salts that make up the bone and sinews of your body.

One day, a straggler from the '60s founding group of the original New Age Foundation, of which I was the freeloading caretaker, shows up in our front yard. Doctor Bob was a big, fat, flim-flam man, plain and simple. He was about 275lbs, 5' 7," and balding under his large, brown cowboy hat. He wore a silver belt buckle with some cosmic astrological symbols on it and a western cut sport jacket. He was around 55 or so, and had just married a little old lady named Caroline Hawlsey. She was about twelve or fifteen years his senior and had some dough. In fact, it was she who had donated the money to Colonel Wayne Aho's New Age Foundation to purchase the Mine Office Building I was living in.

This guy reminded me of the lead character in *The Music Man*. He steps out of a blue Buick Electra and sucks in a breath of air, then walks up to me and introduces himself:

"Hello!" He was loud. "I'm Doctor Bob..." and he handed me a cheap card that looked like it was made at home—with magic healing hands on it, sending sparks from the fingers, with the words *The Healing Hands of*

Doctor Bob and a post box in New Mexico somewhere on it, no phone number, no address.

Bob explained that he was affiliated with *The New Age Foundation* and he was here to give a lecture on the twelve basic mineral salts. I insisted we all needed to hear it because it was very important.

We chit chatted some, then Caroline got out of the car and came into the library to look for some books she said were hers that she wanted. She found a booklike volume of old 45 records with recordings of a direct conversation with aliens on a space ship. These were the first real nut cases I had met in a while, but what was so funny to me, was that they were little ole blue hair nut cases, not hippie dopers nut cases. These folks were genuine fruitcakes.

Well, I went and talked to Milton and we arranged to have a meeting in the Community Center at the hotel. It was a warm summer evening; about eight people showed up, which was a pretty good turnout for Triumph.

There was a folding card table center room, with chairs in a circle around it. On the table was a purplish-red silk tablecloth with gold brocade tassels. In the center of the table was a brass horn, like the megaphone a cheerleader would have used in the 30s. Also, to the right of the table was an art easel with a painting of an Indian chief in full headdress. This was a cheap, paint-by-numbers canvas, about 16 x 20 inches in a simple frame.

We were all in our twenties, and not prepared for this medicine show. Doc Bob gave each of us a business card, and began to explain that we were all deficient in at least one or two of the twelve basic mineral salts that make up our bones. There were methods of healing certain health problems by taking these salts, and he was prepared to provide these salts at a rock-bottom fair price at the end of the lecture, show, or whatever kind of hocus pocus bullshit he was about to put us through.

Remember, we had no TV in Triumph in the '70s, so this was big doin's. Doctor Bob continued to explain that he was going into a trance-like state and the spirit of the long dead chief would be speaking to us through him. He was a medium. So... He starts this chanting kind of rhythmical spiel and he begins to work his magic: his big belly starts moving around and his voice, beginning at a low whisper and growing in an ever-loudening frenzy. Then his tone got deeper, like a different voice altogether; I guess the chief was in the house now. So the chief breaks into a different beat, like a war drum—and Bob, or the chief, I'm not sure at this point—starts going around our circle and laying his healing hands on our foreheads and chanting the salts we needed. I guess the chief knew, I mean, he was a chief and all. "Sodium chloride," he shook my head in a rather violent manner to emphasize the magnitude of this revelation. "Magnesium chloride." Then he placed his hand on my equally skeptical neighbor, Allan Heath. And so went the meeting, a total show that was entertaining and certainly different for a weekday night.

I forgot my wallet, so I couldn't buy the sodium chloride the chief told me I needed, but I planned on salting my food more from then on. Salt is important.

The next day Bob showed up on our doorstep and informed me that he had married Caroline Hawsley and was taking over her affairs. As such, we needed to start paying rent. I couldn't help but notice that Caroline had a new black eye that she didn't have yesterday and was keeping crouched down in the big ol' car...

"Get the fuck out,' I said. "Really?"

He said I needed to pay him 150 bucks.

"Really..." I said again with my best New Jersey Accent: "Get ... the ... fuck ... out."

He got the message... and did.

Over the next few days, I was able to track down Caroline's sons in Minnesota and called them. They were successful ranchers, and had their own plane. I explained that I thought their mom was in trouble, and told them that it looked like the "Healing Hands of Doctor Bob" had come down a little too hard on the ol' gal. They flew right out and took over her affairs.

April and I bought the house for 15,000 bucks and made a payment of 130 per month to her, and another 130 to Colonel Wayne, for 10 years. Caroline moved to Islamorada, Florida and I sent the checks there, until one day we got a letter from her son notifying us that she had passed.

Colonel Wayne had a trailer park with a designated "saucer landing pad" up in Tacoma somewhere. He must have waited for the spaceships for the rest of his life.

April and I settled into our home and I began to think about a family.

The Getty Project.

Rupert was truly enjoying having the Getty crew on his mountain. Not only was the money good, but they picked up a lot of loose paper ends that he was not aware of. One concerned the Crown Point claim that my shop was on. The Department of Interior had a law that a patented claim would not be granted if it abutted a farm homestead lot.

The Triumph Mining Company purchased the 24-acre farm parcel that I had been taking my top soil from that abutted the Crown Point claim. Next to the Crown Point was the Silver Crown claim.

In the rush to march to war in 1940, some little things were left undone; a simple matter of paperwork. Being as the company owned the homestead parcel, it was agreed that the request for a patent would be granted. A letter was written to the state capital and a bureaucratic show of support was received; then war was declared and everyone got so busy that they forgot about it.

As time went on and the BLM (Bureau of Land Management) and other government agencies grew more powerful, they chose not to approve the patent.

A patent is a deed, verses an unpatented claim, which is a lease. The difference would cost the BLM millions in the future, but right now, Rupert was collecting rent on a shop that the company built on land it thought it owned, but didn't, because some bureaucrat dropped the ball on the patent request.

So the Strategic Metals program loaned money for improvements on land that The Department of the Interior owned, not a big deal in the scheme of things in 1940. The country was unified in stimulating the economy, no matter what the real cost. Getty and the drill team had a very good theory as to where the vein dipped on East Fork. They re-leased all the Annie group of 55 claims, almost 1,000 acres to the west of Triumph Gulch and discovered a reserve of about 300,000 tons of minable ore. That isn't a lot in mining terms, but Dave Mako, the head geologist, was confident there was more, deeper. They had only received budget for holes to 1,000 feet and in the middle of the project, the Getty Company was purchased by Pennzoil. This was an oil play, a Wall Street deal, and the mining division was whacked off and sold.

Most of the records from the division were given to the University of Wyoming, School of Mines, and can be viewed there. I spent a few hours there and was amazed at the holdings that Getty had, all over the world, and in every state of the union; in gas, oil, fertilizers, coal and minerals of all types.

The amount of data we have on our in-ground resources is staggering. Getty leased the Triumph project to a Canadian company called Bear Creek. They keep it for two years, paid the rents to me and fees to Rupe. Then they flipped it to another company called Ventures West. They sent me a letter saying they would no longer need to rent my buildings.

I had been living in the Pyramid house. I'd had the time and money to finish it, and it was very comfortable.

In those 3 or 4 years I read 100 books, so having no TV was a blessing. I had rents coming in that made my nut. I had the band, and I sold dirt in the summer and plowed snow in the winter. I still recall sitting in the sun room in the dead of winter, next to the pot belly stove, just reading and waiting for the snow to fall.

Sometimes it would be weeks with no snow to plow, so I just read. There was one year, '76 or '77, that it never snowed, so I got a pair of speed skates and went out on the tailings pond, and built a fire. Some of the neighbors showed up with the kids and we had a great time. It was one of those spontaneous moments that you never forget. Those were some of my favorite years in Triumph. There was friction, and a fear that the mine would open that neighbors didn't like, but everyone was working on the big Sun Valley and Ketchum homes so they all had food on their tables.

The old Crazy Horse building was turned into the health food store and, ironically, April ran it and gained a following of women who wanted to use natural birth control methods. I was so busy working that I didn't really understand what was happening. I thought we were trying to have kids. We were trying a lot, but I was blind to what was really happening.

Our little house had a front flower bed full of Tansy. April had big glass jars of Blue Cohosh, Pennyroyal, and Thistle. She was always making tea with those ingredients and adding honey. This was a very old herbal birth control program. There were always women coming over and she was constantly bagging up a mix of that stuff for them.

After the health food store shut down, she got a job as a waitress in Hailey. April was a pretty girl and she made good money as a waitress, but she wanted more out of life.

One day she came home from work and announced that she was going to go to Nursing School in Twin Falls. I was so caught up in my machines and the quarry, the Band, the mine, I just said "fine." What else could I say? She had her mind made up.

April had lots of male admirers and about this time, she began to let me know it. It was subtle at first, but one night after we made love, I told her I loved her and how we would be together when we were old and gray.

"You never know," was her response.

She was packing her bags and I was too stupid to think she would leave. Milton had married us in his living room, and we placed our hands on his Bible. I gave her a Gumby ring from a Cracker Jack's box. She thought that was cool and unmaterialistic, but really we were just playing house.

Around this time of prosperity, a dark cloud began to form over Triumph. The glory days were fading and the first TV satellite dish found its way up East Fork to the one of the Triumph houses. Once people began to get TV, the social fabric changed very quickly. Within a year, people began to clique up; we didn't visit like we did, we began to play less music together, and it became a different place.

Getty Mining Company | P. O. Box 7900, Salt Lake City, Utah 84107-0900 • Telephone (801) 263-3850

May 29, 1984

Mr. Carl Massaro
Mountain Road Company
Triumph/Hailey, Idaho 83333

Dear Carl:

      Attached is a new service contract for your upcoming work on the
Mascot and Triumph Projects. If you find the contract satisfactory, please
sign the first and last copies and keep the first copy for your records. I'll
pick up the rest when I stop by sometime around June 5th. 'Til then, take
care.

Sincerely,

David A. Mako
Geologist

DAM:dl

A growing government.

Rupert was put on the all new planning commission, representing East Fork Road. The formation of a planning commission in 1977 was a radical new idea, and many people didn't like it. I was at the very first meeting in the old Blaine County courthouse. There was a rancher from down by Gannet that was the chairman. I think his name was Sweat.

"We want to keep this simple," he promised. "We just want a few rules to keep things in check."

Water and ditches were a number one issue down valley; they couldn't have new people or developers messing with water.

At the time, I was planning a small solar project with Milton's blessing. My little house was going to be a model; I wanted to put twelve very small homes along the road on the upper tailings, and turn the rest of the tailings into a park for soccer and baseball. I did the best drawing I could on my drafting board and submitted it with a $250 fee to the new Planning Department, run by a young gal named Meredith Sandler.

Now, Meredith went to college somewhere and studied planning. So did I. But textbook planning is kind of like art; what one person likes, another might hate. Then the real world steps into the office, and often it all goes to hell.

Meredith was in her late twenties and out to save the world from itself. Having been in the county for almost a year, and thanks to her extensive textbook experience, she was going to straighten things out for us.

Now I had only been in Blaine County for 5 or 6 years by then, so I was certainly no authority on things. But Rupe was, and I listened intently to what he had to say.

Blaine County is a very hard climate to make a living in. The cold is so hard on machines and it takes a lot of time to just stay warm in the winter. Not much grows. It's prone to fires in summer, and jobs are far and few between.

Both coasts, especially California, had just come off a ten-year roll of tract development, mountain moving, highway widening, and commercial expansion. Then the recession of '73 hit and construction slowed down.

Now construction in the '70s was the white man's world. We learned drafting in school and shop. I studied Architecture starting in seventh grade, and took it all through high school. Our line work in class was perfect. Hour after hour on a drawing board, we did details and cross hatching, sitting at a drafting table. I grew to hate it; I wanted to be out in the fresh air, standing on a ridge beam. Other guys liked the desk.

At first it didn't matter. Most counties allowed (and many still do) a man to build one house a year, submit his own drawings, and make an honest living. The engineers can deal with the big stuff, three stories and up, or shopping malls, roads, bridges, and airports. Every school in America was teaching drafting and building skills to young men. The thought of an engineer for a one or two-story stick frame home was just incomprehensible to me or any of the friends I knew. To be a builder was a very honorable trade, just below a dentist or lawyer. But there was a wind shift that I didn't see coming.

Don't Californicate Idaho!

NIMBY, 'Not In My Back Yard.' Last one in lock the door! This was the tone that soon took hold in Blaine County, and once the ball got rolling, there was no turning back.

Meredith rented a cheap little crapper of a house, south of Greenhorn Gulch, and moved in with her girlfriend who was also working in the new Planning Department. There was a small asphalt and sand plant a few hundred yards from there that would operate only in summer, and provided the paving for most of Sun Valley and north.

In those days, the state highway department would look for aggregate sources every ten or twelve miles if they could. They would usually pull sand out of the river after the spring runoff, pile it, bring in a small portable crusher, and run it for a week or two and leave the crushed rock material in a few sizes in stockpiles. Then, when winter came, they had sand to spread on the roads and gravel for repairs. This was how things worked for many years, and it left a swimming hole in the river for the summer that would be filled with new sand from the mountains every spring.

When the asphalt plant was running, Meredith could smell it. So she laid plans to shut it down. The master plan that she was working on put all sand and gravel down in the Belleview Triangle.

I was selling material to that plant. The owner would mix one load of Triumph fines with two loads of river sand. He explained to me that, under a magnifying glass, the Triumph fines are sharp plates, so they lay down flat within the round river sand and make a smoother surface for the bike paths and tennis courts.

There were a couple different types of materials left over by the mining operations: coarse rock in the dump, about 250,000 yards, and fines that fall through a quarter-inch screen, 30,000 yards. That material was reworked dump rock. It was reprocessed in the sixties by Federal Resources Corporation. They went through the old dumps and re-crushed, washed, and removed more gold, silver, lead and zinc from the dumps' overburden Between 1964 and 1968 that reworked about 30,000 yards of the Triumph Dump and recovered about 5,000 ounces of gold, 20,000 onces of silver and a bunch of lead and zinc.

What remained was washed flakes of black shale. I sold that and paid Rupe his royalty of twenty-five cents per yard. It added up to four or five hundred per month.

Then there were the tailings. The tailings are the fine sand and slimes that go through a one-sixteenth inch screen. The upper tails from the North Star stamp mill, built in 1889, were a bit coarser; and the lower tails from the newer sink float mill, built in 1952, still have the gold left because the funding for that mill came from Roosevelt era; by 1945, they were working behind the scenes to get away from the gold standard and saw no need to get more of it into circulation.

There was still a need for lead in aircraft fuel, but by 1955, that would change because aircraft began to shift to jet fuel. By 1957, lead was worth about half the 1945 price, from eighteen cents to ten cents. The mine was going to close, and it did. What was left behind was what I made a living from.

Meredith cut into my bread and butter, helped put an end to swimming holes on the river, and put that little asphalt company out of business.

Others might see it differently, but what I saw was an entry-level bureaucrat with the power to hurt me and she did. But she was a nice person.

She got a paycheck, as well as healthcare insurance. I had planned on living forever so I didn't need that. When I was young, I was a runner. I raced in a lot of races on the East Coast. I love to run, and you learn a lot about sticking when you run. I stick; I slow down sometimes, but I stick.

Zoning?

Now zoning law makes the argument about Miss O'Leary's cow in the great Chicago Fire, and how if there is not regulation, society suffers in general. It is important for us all as a group to be regulated for our own good.

Here I draw parallels to 15th century Tuscany. What was once the center of high art, music, and culture used a form of twisted religious doctrine to ultimately control output of a dutiful population until they revolted. The result was a bloodbath that lasted 100 years.

My great-grandparents left what I think are the most beautiful and productive lands on earth because of oppression by a central controlled doctrine. This correlation between beliefs and rights is where we are again.

In 1950, the Federal Government began a program to house the GIs and Levittowns sprung up all over America. I grew up in a small Levittown home that cost $12,000 at 3%. After fifteen years on that note, my pop still owed $9,000.00. That's the hideous result of a mortgage; millions and millions of working families struggling to pay interest on money used to build a shelter.

Rupert, on the other hand, built his shelter out of recycled wood, salvaged from the mine. It was for all intents and purposes a shack, not much better than the shacks I saw in Haiti. But for the prime youthful years of his family life, he was not slaving to pay interest of a fiat currency mortgage. Fiat currency means a paper currency that is not backed by commodities (gold and silver), but works by ever-expanding the supply, charging interests on that expanding supply, and taxing what appears on the surface to be profit, but, in regards to real estate, really isn't.

You can almost never buy back a property for less than what you sell it for unless there is a depression, where the banks fail and call in notes.

When you're young and all your animal impulses are driving you to procreate, most young people can't save much. To save up $10,000 dollars as a laborer or waitress is practically impossible.

As government expands its tentacles of control in an effort to protect us, fees, permits, licenses, and costs associated with compliance of these rules slowly begin to creep into daily life—until the cement sets up, until none but the richest folks can comply or rise above it all.

This leaves the rest of the population struggling for scraps, blaming each other for this or that. I had very little money, but I put it all back into better tools and equipment.

My first little house was a shack, a goat shed, but it was mine. If I wanted to padlock the door and do a *walkabout*, I could. Most families are too tied to the fire.

Let's look at a small part of the material stream that goes onto the structure we call the American Home. In 1952, when a logging company cut a tree down, the logger got paid by the stumpage. He cut down the tree and hauled it to the mill; the tree is cut, dried, inspected for grade, and shipped to a lumber yard in your home town. These lumber yards usually worked with a larger regional wholesaler linked to a rail site.

As the population grows, demands and restrictions on that supply chain increase. Nobody wants more sprawl and choking growth squeezing in line for a piece of the pie. With a fiat currency, each family constantly needs more dollars to buy that loaf of bread. So, much like a fraternity, we screw the new guy. The problem with this concept is one day you get no more new guys wanting to join this crappy fraternity and the hall closes—or you get dumber and dumber new guys wanting to join because way back when, somebody of note was a member.

So, back to our lumber board; by now it has to contribute to fire management, soil conservation, OSHA's safety rules, pensions, trucking regulations, EPA and wildlife studies, raising insurance, zoning and legal fees, lending regulations, inspections, engineering and architectural, as well as contractors' fees—such as licenses, bonds, and on and on. That simple board that comes off the sawmill carriage and lands on the rollers might cost twenty cents, but by the time it gets into the wall of your home, its three bucks and you pay for thirty years at 5% or 6% on that board.

We have a government-controlled system of housing that isn't really government at all, because the lenders are not government; they are fiat bankers. This system keeps our young families in perpetual slavery. The stress related to just keeping a roof over the family vents in so many other ways, often in broken homes.

About 40% of the buildings standing in this country were built before 1949. In my humble opinion, they are better built than most new buildings; just less energy efficient. Does a constant 72-degree temperature for a human being make them stronger or weaker? I could make an argument that climate control weakens the population and these new, tighter homes have caused an explosion in asthma related problems for the residents. Now with cable TV, we can all stay in, glued to the box.

Rupert and Milton, as different as they were, had that do-it-yourself, no mortgage home in common. To live your whole life in a shack on fifty acres of your own land, or ten, or one, might be better than working thirty years to pay off a Fannie or Freddy loan. Hell, the hospital or nursing home liens it when you get old, so many Americans are left with nothing.

The Survey.

There were problems with the survey. The Wooden Hill survey was recorded in 1972. There was no zoning, no review, no checking, and the Triumph Mining Company was not notified or in any way consulted on changes to the original plat.

The original plat was a group of mill site claims, centered on the Baby Ethel Mill site and a fire system. The North Star road was cut off by Bill Karst, when he put his mother-in-law Hulda's trailer in his front yard. Hulda owned a few buildings that Ernie left her, including the big barn that was the ore car manufacturing shed, and the tin building that was the pipe threading and air tool repair shop.

Dan Tucker bought the barn in 1974 for ten grand, and I bought the pipe shop in 1977 for seventeen. We were once close, but now we don't talk.

Dan went into the fence business and fenced in 10 or 15 feet of the 66-foot easement the mine retained in East Fork Road, thereby making his yard bigger. And when I called him on it, the county killed the messenger and fined me for marking it. Then he and Gordon, the local surveyor, filed for a road shift, and took twelve by one hundred and twenty feet of my pipe shop's lot.

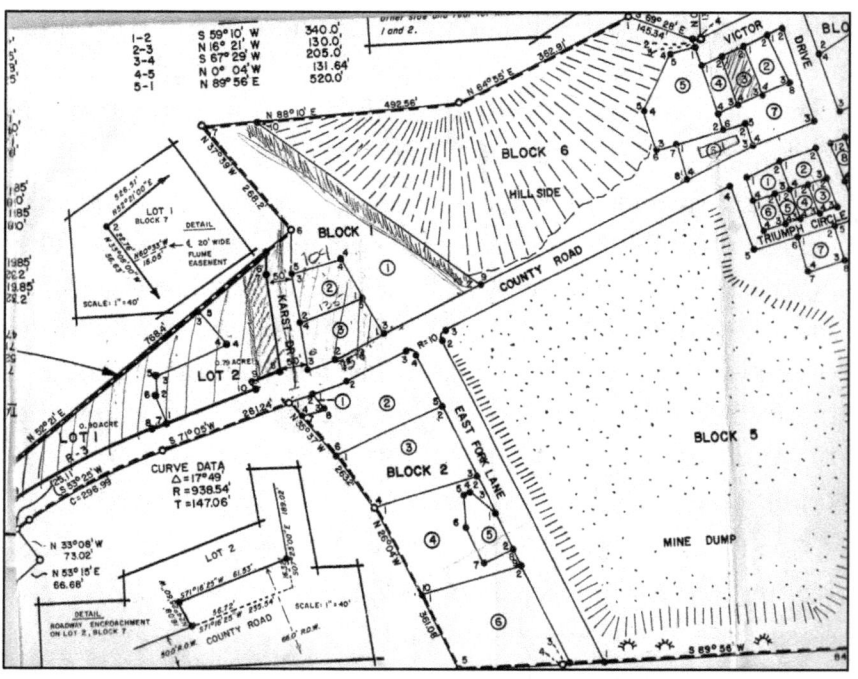

Before that, Gordon and Jim Bradford resurveyed my end of town and shifted every lot line 28 feet to the west, almost closing off the road to the entire mine property. They did this while Ken Rabbee, the resident of the adjoining land, was in the hospital flat on his back after a nasty fall on a jobsite and could not be there to protest it.

The flower power was wearing off. The sales agreement with Harr's Lutheran group clearly stated in simple language that "the mine retained the rights to use all roads, as well as mineral rights and tailings thereon." But as time went on, folks began to push and challenge that. Land trusts began to eye the property; as the partners grew older, people swarmed in like vultures and began to pick at the old corporate whale gasping for air.

When Getty was on the hill and they hired me as a subcontractor, we were in control of things. But the neighbors didn't like it, because they had thought the mine would never open and their property would excel like the rest of Sun Valley real estate.

Milton had sold these little houses for six or seven thousand to anyone who came along, no questions no credit application; 10% down, 10% interest, 10 years to pay. The people that got a foot on the ladder of home ownership would have never made it without that start. The flip side of that, in hind sight, was that Milton would have died a penniless pauper had it not been for the flower children that came along to buy him out.

Today in Blaine County there are few opportunities like that, none like Triumph. Today the young workers who don't have a trust fund are likely to end up in a public housing program run by a democratic machine. The Housing Authority shakes down the developers of upper middle class homes, and forces them to contribute to a kitty for the poor. This system is so prone to corruption, because they won't give the developer a permit if he doesn't play ball. This is a long way from the freedoms that settled the West. I think a better system would have been to allow a second unit on the big houses at a tax break—thereby providing starter housing, lowering the cost to the taxpayers and providing a caretaker culture to the big homes that are empty most of the time. This economy is doomed unless Blaine County can undo much of what they did in the '80s, but to do so will be difficult.

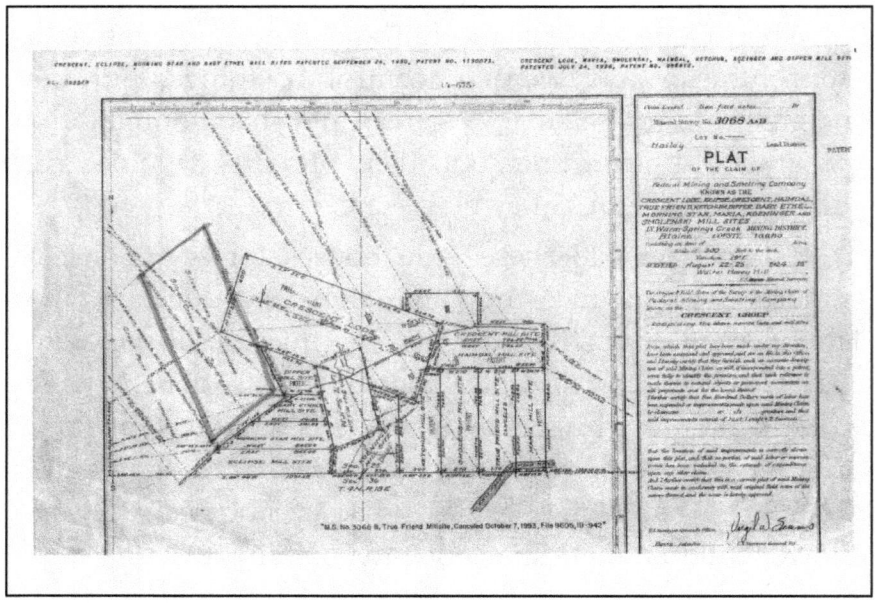

"Honey, come look."

April had been using all kinds of herbal birth control teas, roots, and potions to avoid having a child. I was so self-absorbed in keeping my trucks running and making my equipment payments, I didn't even know it—until one day, she was in the bathroom, calling, "Look it worked, it really worked!"

I came in to see a little bloody gob in the toilet. It took a few moments for it to sink in. Was this a four-week-old fetus, getting flushed down the drain? Our relationship took a big hit that day.

She wanted to go to Boise to do pre-med; change the world and save the American medical system. She talked her best friend Wendy into going. Wendy was having trouble in her marriage as well. There are bumps that form down the nuptial pike.

The two headed off to Boise, leaving Bill and me having to get used to being bachelors. Bill had his big blue bus, set up as a camper. We took it down there and they set up house together in a trailer park near Boise State.

Things didn't go well between them. I got April's side of the story, but never Wendy's. It seemed that Wendy was having trouble with Organic Chemistry, and April was making new study group friends that were grasping it better. A competition developed between the two old friends. Soon Wendy would tell April she heard a voice that told her to go back to Triumph and return to her faith, much like the path of Emanuel Swedenborg who spent his early years studying the sciences, then heard his calling and turned to his Lord.

Wendy came home to Triumph to meditate on life and to rekindle the peace and tranquility of East Fork, only to hear the noise and smell the smoke from my old diesel loader and trucks. I had those damn OSHA-mandatory back up buzzers on my machines and I was working my ass off to come up with the ten grand-plus it took to put April through school.

Wendy was a very pretty, persuasive person. If she were to knock on your door all dolled up, you would let her in to hear what she had to say. Well, she waxed up the BMW, put on her diamond earrings, and headed down East Fork Road with a petition to shut me down.

I had filed on a quarry on a state parcel that was down by the river near the cave I first camped at. There was an old river crossing there to the tunnel and the logging the mine did on the mountain we called Mind Bender. The rock slide held several hundred thousand tons of building stone, and some large boulders at the bottom of the rock pile surrounded by very tall cottonwood trees. I wanted my own quarry, to not haul for Stubby anymore because the road to his quarry was a truck killer. I had snapped two huge axles and almost went over, and the excitement of the climb had faded to a blur of bad truck repairs.

The quarry at the river had good stone and was so much easier on the machines. I still had to load by hand, twelve tons per load, but when the spring floods came that year, houses along the river in Gimlet were in danger of washing away and rip rap was hard to come by.

I got a desperate call from a lady on Warms Springs Road, just south of the bridge. She was losing her yard and was afraid she was going to lose her house. My trusty old military five-ton 6x6 liked driving in high water; these trucks were built for National Guard service in flood zones, and were designed to run in four or five feet of water. So I broke the terms of my quarrying agreement this one time and took my loader through the crossing to the quarry with my helper, Smitty, driving the truck behind me.

We hauled out five loads of big rock to that Warms Springs home in Ketchum and saved the yard, but Collins got pictures and began to shut me down. That was easy. Every NIMBY on East Fork would gladly sign a petition to stop mining up their road.

I became the demon, nature-hating, money-grubbing truck driver; she was doing the *Lord's work*, saving the land.

I wish I could forgive her, but it looked to me like she was backhandedly attacking her old friend, April, more than me. If the money stopped coming in the door, love would go out the window.

One day I was skiing on Baldy with an old friend, Casey Clark. I hadn't seen Casey in years; she had married a French man and moved to Paris. She was back in Sun Valley for Christmas break, and we were skiing together. I was just getting off the chair on top of Baldy, getting my poles on, adjusting my glasses, being really cool when I caught an edge in some soft stuff and fell forward—very slowly, hard on my shoulder, dislocated it bad, really bad. They took me off the hill in a sled to the hospital in Sun Valley. There they popped it back in, shot me up with morphine, and let me out.

Casey stayed with me the whole way, and I've never seen her since. She drove me out to Triumph to my little pyramid house. When we got there, April was boxing up her things and moving out. She was going to leave me a letter. *Dear Carl,* it read, *I love you, but I don't want to be married to a truck driver. I want more out of life and being married to you and owning this house makes it impossible to get a college loan. I don't want anything. You will find someone better for you than me, Love April Haug.*

She handed me the letter, loaded her things, and as she left, Casey said, "Nice to meet you."

"Well, you have had a busy day." She knew I was in trouble.

Casey got me into my chair, built a fire in the stove, and said goodbye. I've never seen her again, but I sure hope I get to thank her someday...

I was a broken man. The shoulder hurt more than any other pain I've ever had. It was a deep kind of pain, kind of like a combination of nerve tingles and black-and-blue pain magnified times ten.

I began to drink more and smoke dope, reefer. I let my trucks go, stopped spending money on maintenance and tires. Big trucks cost a lot to keep running; often the owner can find himself making the choice between tires and food. I had become very thin, too—170 lbs, too thin for me. I was falling and I didn't care. I didn't care about anything.

Harry Dean Stanton   Bill Janss   Carl Massaro   George Gund III

July 1976
Levi Strauss Western Movies: Myths & Images

Wall Street comes knocking.

Rupert was about to fall into a bit of a rut. Although he was on the top of his game, and chairman of the County Commission, he was about to lose a big part of the revenue from Getty when, once again, Wall Street came knocking at the door.

In the summer of 1984, Pennzoil was drilling for oil on Wall Street. That is to say, they bid to buy 51% of the Getty Oil Company, 40% owned by Grandpa Getty and 11% held by the Getty Museum Trust. Pretty smart, you put the controlling shares in a big, nonprofit, personal castle, full of art that you charge folks to see.

So Getty entered into an agreement to give Pennzoil an option to purchase these shares at $108 each. Pennzoil has a party, but by the time the champagne is finished, Getty gets a better offer from Texaco for $125 per share.

Getty sells to Texaco and fully expects to honor the option for Pennzoil, netting a tidy 120 million for Pennzoil, but that's chump change. Pennzoil sues Getty, requests a summary judgment, and the case drags on for three long years. In the end, Texaco forks up three billion in a settlement.

All that time, Getty was paying rent to me for the thousands of boxs of core in the shop out in Triumph, and paying a portion of their rent to Rupe in a renegotiated deal. But the work stopped: the drilling and road building, the research and data collection.

Getty's team had amassed a huge collection of data on the mine, and Rupe asked me if he could store it in the vault: maps, log books, pay records, all the papers from 1888 to 1959, letters from the Philadelphia Company, the Hearsts' mines, Ivanhoe Mines, the San Louis Mining Company, the Federal Mining and Smelting Company—a corporate Who's Who of American mining. Why did they leave, and where did they go? This topic fascinates me so I have studied and continue to follow it.

Hard currency vs. paper.

Rupert once tried to explain to me the difference between a dollar made from investing and a dollar pulled out of the ground. When a miner digs in the earth and pulls out a pound of mineral and puts it into circulation, it begins to become products, hard goods, that create jobs, produce revenue, and those products generate taxes, etc. There's an old New England proverb: "Firewood heats you twice." Once when you cut it, and once when you burn it.

When the Federal Reserve creates debt, it prints bonds that are backed by the taxes collected from the citizens of that country, and creates a very, very, different kind of financial cycle.

A pound of silver does not change. It's a rock solid inert mineral. You could place it in King Tut's tomb and come back five thousand years later and it's still silver.

But if you were to take a pound of paper US dollars, put them in a time capsule, and come back in five thousand years, you would have a pound of toilet paper, maybe.

Now financial wizards will tell you that we have a higher standard of living, the modern world moves too fast for a bimetal money system, blah, blah, blah. Maybe so, after 5,000 years of gold-backed currency; the past 100 years of fiat currency have built a very fast-paced modern world. If you can, view fiat currency as a flowing river delta, ever moving forward and expanding, all the while the water gets shallower and shallower. When the ship hits bottom, you wait, stranded until the spring rains come and push you a little further, only to have it happen again downstream.

World powers have always gained their strength from minerals, crops and timber, but mostly from minerals. The Bronze Age begat the Steel Age. The oil age would never have happened without drill steel. It's minerals that are the flow behind the paper banking curtain we see.

But over a period of ten short years, minerals in America found a new kind of hooded enemy knocking on their door, demanding payment and protection money.

Now, please don't get me wrong here. I was on the clear water sloop, supporting cleaning up the Hudson River where GE had been dumping god-knows-what into it for fifty years. The quiet killer flowed down only to mix with New York City's sewage and out to sea. I spent a summer building houses on Tom River, where CIBY dumped horrible stuff in leaky lagoons with a sand bottom. But the EPA were bullies, and industry dug their heals in; so in the late '80s, the govenment came down hard on so many American factories that were already beginning to feel the heat of the industrial forges in Asia. Instead of working with industry, they fined it into bankruptcy.

The flash flood on Eastfork.

It was the spring of 1984. A big flood washed out the bridge up East Fork, past Triumph. Some folks got stuck on the other side.

Rupe was chairman of the County Commission then, and had been on the Hailey Road Department for several years prior, so he acted quickly. They hauled a very large eight-foot round by twenty-foot culvert up there, and told road boys to grab waste rock from my screen at the mine dump to hold it in. The water was rushing, but it had slowed from the flash flood. And the waste rock had some large chunks that would provide a solid fill for the pipe. They got it done fast and the folks got out. The road was opened, and the plan was to put the bridge back in summer.

Residents of triumph who supported the campaign to stop my rock quarry, and hated my gravel operation, contacted the EPA regional office and complained about the Road Department dumping that *toxic* mine waste into the river.

Now you need to understand something here. The Milligan Rock Formation is a huge geological superstar. It runs from Bolder City well north of Ketchum, down to the southwest side of Bellevue at the Silver Queen Mine; billions upon billions of tons of black rock with white and red veins run through it.

Every spring the rivers wash it downstream, have done so for ages, and will continue to do so. The rock in the dump was black county rock that the miners determined had no valuable metal, so they put it on *the Dump*. It had traces, as did any rock in the whole region. The EPA came in and read the county the riot act. "Remove the culvert rock immediately, replace it with lava rock or large river rock, and take that *toxic* rock to the dump. Dispose of it like it was radioactive waste. The orders came down from the Feds.

Rupert was furious. It cost the taxpayers money, it made him look bad, and it was stupid.

This was just the beginning. Rupert had pissed off some young buck looking to make his bones, so Rupe became his mark. After somone called on the bridge, the EPA had Triumph on their radar. I wonder who it was? They were bound to find it anyway because they had money, lots of it, allotted to clean up lead mines from Telluride to Canada. The entire Rocky Mountain region was known for its *black shales*.

These black shales got hot long ago and precipitated heavy metals into veins. They contained silver, lead, zinc, and gold, with traces of copper. They built the west, only to become villainized by the very same federal government that funded their exploration eighty years earlier.

The EPA was an offshoot of the Department of the Interior, as were the Strategic Metals Department and the Department of Mines and Minerals. There was an internal federal turf war going on, and The Triumph Mineral Company got caught up in it. This was beyond crazy, and I will always believe that the crippling of our Galena mines had more to do with silver and gold, and now ammunition, than lead safety.

As more and more wealthy people began to move into the Valley, land trusts became popular. They were trendy, tax exempt, and provided a social status for the New Money, who were educated and really didn't want to join the Hailey Rotary or the Grange to mix with the simple farm and ranch folk. They wanted to support art auctions and dressage events.

Oh, they might go slumming on Rodeo Weekend or Wagon Days, break out those cowboy clothes, and play the part. But they were going to 'save' the land, and that meant taking it from those families that had been here for the past 100 years. It was war, and there would be blood. The EPA finished the work that local NIMBY's started and my trucking business was shut down; so was the top soil. Rumored to have lead, my sales fell to nothing. I was broke.

Here comes the bill.

Rupert had worked very hard in Blaine County; he had risen through the ranks of government, from 4-H, soil conservation, sheriff's posse, Rodeo Commission, Grange, County Commission, and Airport Commission. He had received a plaque and letter from the Governor for his service to the state of Idaho.

One day he received a letter from a law office in Seattle. *Dear Mr. House, the Clean Water Act, blah, blah, section number, blah, blah, mine discharge, owners of mines, etc... Your share of the cleanup is 4.7 million dollars.*

Now I don't care how tough you are, that will rattle your cage.

The main portal of the Triumph taps into the underground river that flooded the lower levels in 1939. The water that comes out picked up the oxidation from the iron sulfides and pyrites, and was about as acidic as lemon juice. It was 55 degrees, and flowed year-round at a steady rate of 100 gallons per minute. We calculated; with its fall, it could produce 57 horsepower.

The EPA held the Federal Mining and Smelting Company responsible for the expense as well as fines, even though 30 years earlier, the same Department of the Interior gave the company loans to build the mine for the war effort.

DO4 ROBIdS-801-263-9000
FX. 261-2194

HELLER EHRMAN WHITE & McAULIFFE

ATTORNEYS
A PARTNERSHIP OF PROFESSIONAL CORPORATIONS

DEAN NIGARD

ROB HANSON
208/313-0290
888-800-8480

6100 COLUMBIA CENTER
701 FIFTH AVENUE
SEATTLE
WASHINGTON 98104-7098
TELEPHONE: (206) 447-0900
FACSIMILE: (206) 447-0849

MARCIA NEWLANDS
(206) 389-6102
mnewlands@hewm.com

May 29, 1998

SEATTLE
PORTLAND
TACOMA
ANCHORAGE

SAN FRANCISCO
LOS ANGELES
PALO ALTO

WASHINGTON, D.C.
HONG KONG
SINGAPORE

16004-0064

Via FedEx

Mr. Rupert House
President
Triumph Mineral Company, Inc.
308 East Fork Road
Hailey, ID 83333

Mr. Bus House
2107 South Stearns
Oakdale, CA 95361

        Re: **Triumph Mine Portal, Triumph Mine Site, Idaho**

Dear Rupert and Bus:

        First, on behalf of Asarco, we want to thank you for meeting with Lands and Asarco in Ketchum in March. We appreciate your taking the time to discuss the Triumph remediation.

        At that meeting, you asked for an explanation of Asarco's position concerning obligations under the law for remediation and maintenance of the Triumph Mine and the portal discharge. Asarco's position is as follows.

        Under Section 107 of CERCLA, 42 U.S.C. § 9607, which is also referred to as the Superfund Law, the owner or operator of a facility where hazardous substances are present, is liable for, among other things, the cost of removal or remediation of the hazardous substances at the site. At the Triumph site, this includes activities undertaken at the mine portal related to remediation or control of the water discharging from the mine. According to the remedial investigation undertaken at the site, the mine portal water contains elevated levels of metals that the EPA and DEQ believe may pose a threat to human health or the environment. The DEQ, supported by the EPA, is requiring the discharge be controlled or remediated by the PRPs. Triumph Mineral Company is a PRP at the site that DEQ and EPA may hold liable for the discharge.

In addition to its authority under CERCLA, the EPA also claims authority over the mine discharge under the Clean Water Act, 33 U.S.C. §§ 1251 et seq. The EPA is authorized to establish water quality standards and to enforce those standards by establishing limits on the concentrations of various substances, including metals, in waters that are discharged to the "waters of the United States." The standards are established to protect fish and aquatic life, recreational uses, and public water supplies. Because the waters discharging from the mine portal may ultimately discharge to a stream or to groundwater, the EPA claims the authority to control the quality of the water. This is typically done by issuing a permit to the "owner" of the water source, requiring that the owner undertake whatever reasonable means are necessary to ensure the quality of the water.

In the case of the Triumph Mine portal water, it is Asarco's position that the EPA could issue an NPDES permit, requiring that metals in the water discharged from the mine be at or below certain levels. If the water fails to meet these criteria, the EPA is authorized to issue orders or penalties to compel compliance. Under the Clean Water Act, as the owner of the mine, Triumph Mineral Company is responsible for the water discharging from the mine and, therefore, responsible for the quality of that water.

Briefly, the above is a summary of Asarco's interpretation of the law as it relates to your company's potential obligation for the mine discharge. Under either Superfund or the Clean Water Act, the mine's owners may be liable for the quality of the water.

Asarco and Lands have agreed to undertake the investigation of the site, and to participate in its remediation. However, Asarco is looking to Triumph Minerals to undertake its share of responsibility for the remediation of the site as well. Although the Superfund Law permits parties such as Lands and Asarco to go to court to recover the costs of remediation from other responsible parties, such as Triumph Minerals, Asarco is hopeful that Triumph Minerals Company will be willing to arrive at an arrangement with Asarco outside of court. To that end, Asarco requests that Triumph Minerals contribute funds, or something of equivalent value, to cover the costs of remediating the mine portal and maintaining the mine portal water system once the plug is installed. Depending on the value of what Triumph Minerals is able to offer, Asarco is willing to discuss waiving any future claims of liability against Triumph Minerals.

In addition to undertaking part of the cost of the project, Asarco also requests that Triumph Minerals provide continuous access to the mine portal for Asarco, Lands, and

HELLER EHRMAN WHITE & McAULIFFE
ATTORNEYS

any other PRPs who may have obligations to maintain the portal and its water discharge, and that Asarco and Lands be permitted to install a locked gate at the mouth of the portal and to run pipelines from the portal to a settling pond to be located west of the portal.

You mentioned at one point that Triumph Minerals may be interested in offering land rather than money for its share of the costs. Although Asarco may be willing to accept real estate in lieu of cash, Asarco is not interested in obtaining title to any additional mines or contaminated properties to which Triumph Minerals may hold title.

It is our understanding that your company has not engaged an attorney to represent your company's interests at the site. You both directed me to send this letter to you. However, if you engage an attorney to represent your company's interests at the Triumph Site, which we recommend that you do, I would appreciate your notifying me so that I may communicate directly with your attorney. In the interim, if you wish to discuss any of the above with me, please call me at (206) 389-6102, or Don Robbins of Asarco at (801) 263-5220. We look forward to your response.

Yours very truly,

Marcia Newlands

cc: D.A. Robbins
        J. Chris Pfahl
        Robert Comer
        Michael R. Thorp

51780.01.SE (13YC011.DOC)
05/29/98 12:05 PM

The company followed all the rules. In fact, government contracted geologists did the maps and projections for ore reserves the Strategic Metals Program funded.

I had applied two years earlier, with Rupert's approval, to the state of Idaho for permission to clean the water so we could use it for greenhouses and water power. I dug ponds and ran the water into one while the other dried in the sun. Then I would rake up the red iron oxide and pile it. I took it around to some paint manufactures and brick paver manufacturers who agreed to buy it for eighty five cents per pound, if I could get it dry and screened. I even went to visit the famous architect, Palo Solieri, in Arizona and attempted to trade with him for his green copper sulfate.

A geologist told me that there was about thirty dollars a day in silver coming out in those pigments, so I felt the discharge was a potential asset, particularly from the geothermal angle.

With a real budget, we could have built a system of smooth concrete troughs, thirty inches deep with filter baffles that would remove 90% of the pigment. As we changed the filters, they could be dried and vacuumed into bags.

This would create some jobs and clean the water. Then it could move on to heat the floors in a series of greenhouses, and the condensation between the hot water and the cool air would create enough pure $H2O$ to water the plants in the greenhouse. That would create more jobs. Then, the water would run down the hill in an eight-inch pipe and produce electricity equivalent to 57 hp, 24 hours a day, 365 days a year.

Now, I will be the first to admit, in hindsight, that I was hitting the peace pipe a lot in those days, and the disconnect between political reality and my pipe dreams was huge. But, a simple calculation of the electrical would yield: 100 mph falling 200 ft. = 57 hp. Let's say 60 hp = 100 kWh= about $8 per hour x 24 = $192 per day x 365= about $70,000 per year.

Had we put a generator on that water twenty years ago, it would have produced the equivalent of $1,400,000 in power. Plus the value of oxide, and the greenhouse revenue that may or may not be significant. (Depending on the grower's enthusiasm in a very hard market.)

Point being, the EPA and the IDEQ came on like uncreative thugs that were set on spending the money as quickly as possible. They beat up the old men who were the shareholders of the Triumph Mineral Company, they beat up ASARCO, the descendants of the Federal Mining and Smelting Company, and more importantly, they reneged on every promise they made in the 1940 expansion program that they controlled under the NRA. Now we knew how Geronimo felt; white man definitely speaks with forked tongue.

The total bill for the cleanup was estimated to be about twelve million. That was padded, and I mean really padded, with engineering fees, legal fees, public hearing costs, and litigation between conflicting interests.

After several years of crushing, stressful public meetings that amounted to a witch hunt, the actual work was performed by a small company out of Missoula with a couple of trucks (not much better than mine), an excavator, and a dozer. They were paid about 250 grand. They knocked down all the buildings, and buried the debris on site. That was easy!

ASARCO spent about $500,000 bucks on the tunnel (against Rupert's advice) and received, as payment in full, the best parcel of land that the Triumph Mineral Company had left, the 24-acre farm homestead parcel.

Here is a perfect example of government FUBAR. What we call *the Bench* (see map) was composed of three parcels. The 24-acre homestead;, Silver Crown claim that was recorded in the winter of 1917 from a desk somewhere and later replotted with slightly varied data angles (that led to another set of survey issues); and the Crown Point Claim, that was staked and requested for patent in 1920, but not granted as a patent because there was a federal law that said a patented claim cannot abut a homestead parcel. So, the company bought the homestead parcel and resubmitted for a patent on the Crown Point.

Each of these were about 20 acres, and the machinery rooms with the compressors were built on them with the understanding that the patent would be issued. There were correspondences from senators and government officials to that effect (see photo), but the Feds never give something without a string attached, and in the end, some mid-level bozo decided to drag his feet. Well, 35 years later when the Idaho DEQ went looking to sue responsible parties, they 'ate their own young' and sued the BLM.

The State of Idaho sued the BLM for a million in cleanup costs. There is no logic dealing with federal and state agencies, there is no right or wrong, and they are not your friend. They are a churning, destructive, money machine—constantly calling back to Washington for more, more, more of your tax money.

Had they treated Rupert fairly, the water could be cleaner. The site could have been terraced and planted in pines, which like the zinc, and do well in the dump material if some organic matter is added.

Instead, we have a giant column of water building up behind that plug. At last reading, before the tunnel collapsed on the meter, it was 257 feet at 125 PSI and rising, just as Rupert told them it would.

Now I do not have a degree in geology, but I bet I could take a college-level geology exam and score a 72. I was a rock hound as a kid. I did lapidary work, dozer work, excavation, and read the engineering and mining journal cover to cover for years and still read more from several sites on minerals and exploration. I agreed with Rupe, that the plug was a bad idea in our mountain.

First, you can go online and find several situations worldwide where plugs have failed when the earth shifts. Geology 101, the earth is always, ALWAYS moving. A billion years ago, the black shales were laid down flat. As the Rockies lifted, the flat plates were set on a very steep angle of almost 50 degrees. Then the volcanic party started and the rock got cooked, boiled really, leaving a hard dolomite vein between the ore body and the shale, much like foam on the top of a cold beer. On one side of the dolomite quartz is a galena deposit running uphill at a 50 degree angle, and on the other side is what is called karst rock. When you take a glass marble and put it in boiling water, then toss it in cold water, the glass will crack in every direction. This is what karst does. Much of the rock near the surface in Idaho is karst. As the snow and ice work it over, it falls apart, making these shale slides we see everywhere.

Rupert tried to explain that they were having problems through the years, with cave-ins along the first one thousand feet of the main portal tunnel. That's why Jack Rutter poured that opening with cement in 1952. The tunnel was dug in the 20s, then widened in the early 40s under a federal expansion program. Rupert rode in the damn thing every day for 25 years, and he knew it was prone to cave-ins.

For 15 years, I monitored that water. I knew no matter how big a pipe you place for that water to run through, it will plug it. The iron particles are very, very small; they precipitate and collect on each other. They are so small that when going through a sand or gravel filter, they will plug it, no matter what, and that's what they are doing in the mountain. They are finding their way into the karst rock cracks and plugging them. The water will continue to rise, increasing the pressure behind that plug until there is an event like an earthquake. Then the plates will shift a little, because that's what plates do, and although the plug might stay fastened to the quartz dolomite layer, the tunnel line will shift enough for the water to find its way around it. The water will come out, and it could be a huge rush all at once or 500 gallons a minute for many years.

When that happens, the state will need more money; lots more. They will go after everyone again, myself included, because they gave the Triumph Mineral Company no seat at the table, no opinions, not even the opportunity to participate.

I do not see any honor or integrity dealing with these bureaucracies. Yes, there are men of honor in some of those offices. But when they move as a force and consider the liability as a whole, in relation to them losing their jobs and their pensions and health care for their families and loved ones, we were hurt and so was the Idaho taxpayer.

It would be hard to calculate the volume of water in the main portal, but let me try to put the fear of god in you. An 8 x 8 x 10-foot section of tunnel would be 640 cu ft x 7.5=4800 gal x 6 miles of tunnel. Now that's assuming the tunnel remained the size it was dug in 1940; it didn't. When I went in there in 2005, when I owned the mine, it was 20 feet tall and 25 feet across after years of slowly crumbling. So let's say 20 x 20 x 6 miles = the equivalent of the water in the Wood River from Hailey to Ketchum, sitting in a mountain with a 270-foot column on a fault. Oh, and the feeder tunnels are smaller but many miles long... to paraphrase Forest Gump, "I'm no genius but that might be a prob-lem m."

In Tennessee, a few years back there was a large tailings pond made of coal sludge from a coal fired plant. It was supposed to be safe, and insured, when a big rain event happened—causing it to flood a wash down the river. It put twelve feet of sludge over hundreds of thousands of acres, destroying people's homes and costing billions. The TVA just raised power rates to cover it. I will make this prediction: The state will end up spending far more than they collected screwing around, and never have the guts to admit they were wrong from the start on the tunnel plug. When it blows, they will blame it on the Feds...

Back to college.

In the winter of 2006, I got a call from Bill Rember and Bia Pesic at what was left of the School of Mines at the University of Idaho in Moscow. Bia had advised the state to process the tailings for the gold, and pump them back into the tunnels instead of capping them on the wetlands.

At the time, with gold at $265, the values would have generated about fifteen million and offset the cleanup costs, instead of suing everyone involved like they did.

We have gotten lazy as a nation. Decisions are made by lazy bureaucrats and lawyers who get their manicures done at salons downtown and enjoy going to the mountains in Eddie Bauer clothes on the weekends. I just hope it doesn't devastate East Fork Canyon in the process, but that would get rid of the beaver, they won't live in the iron sulfide water.

A few days before Christmas 2013, I took a walk up onto *the Bench* where the main portal plug is. The water was coming out at around 20 gallons per minute, 4 times what it was when the plug was installed. Before the plug, it ran at 100 gals per minute, but it has been almost twenty years. People forget, and now the state is in charge so they will spend taxpayer money forever.

If I sound negative, it's because it hurts to see potential not only being wasted, but stolen, and the crooks operate from our tax money. When I hear the media rambling on about the pipeline or the coal companies, I wonder how Americans would feel if they really saw what was happening. Minerals and vegetables are what really make the world go around, not money. Money is just a measuring device. I see the EPA's cleanup program in the Rockies, and now the Appalachians, as a control tool to crush any hope of a return to a bimetal currency, a taking of the raw materials for ammunition, and a forced acceptance of government controlled electricity via the nuclear industry. Wind and Solar are just a smoke screen and will only serve to crush enemies of a government-controlled grid.

Go ahead, call me paranoid. I see it clear as day. Like Rupert used to say, "You got to know where you've been to understand where you're going…"

We have entered into a period in this nation where our global competitors are being helped by our own choking regulation and the multinational corporations, many who may connect with the USA, are benefiting while the man on the street sinks deeper and deeper into a kind of subservience to a college loan, and a home mortgage, and soon, higher electricity costs.

Look, Ma, Mt. Bora jumped up!

About 8 years before the EPA came to town, there was a great earthquake in Idaho. The earth vibrated for thirty or forty seconds. So much so that I could hear the trees shaking on Mine Bender across the valley from my shop. This earthquake took Mount Bora, Idaho's largest peak, and shoved it twelve feet into the sky, leaving an earth cliff that ran for a mile at the mountain's base, re-routing underground springs and causing them to pop up miles away in new locations.

Mount Bora is very close, by air, to the Triumph Mine. There is no doubt that the earth will shift along the main tunnel in the Triumph. The hard rock the plug was installed in will continue to slide, slow and steady. Rupert tried to emphasize this to the bullies that came in from the EPA and DEQ. I say bullies, but they were just following orders and Washington is FUBAR. They will spend more money standing behind the decision to plug the portal than the mine produced in the years of operation, because the water will NEVER stop finding ways out. Clearing the water, as I applied for in the 80s, would produce a very small net return, and is easily mocked by bureaucrats, or the new rich that can turn 50 mil by manipulating a stock or pension fund. But in the end, they will spend millions on the plug and its maintenance. I fear the bigger issue will be another earthquake. It isn't *If*, but *when* it breaks and comes out, East Fork will be damaged and people could get hurt. The men in the state offices are good men, and I have known them now for many years. They have aged, as have I, and must go to bed at night feeling they are doing their jobs. They know they could have a big problem but would never admit it for fear of losing their jobs.

What I have seen from my perch on my hill was a transition from private controlled property, to a taking it with fines, and a shift to government controlled property. The fabric of this kind of taking is only a little different than communism or a dictatorship, and it has happened within a generation. It's very dangerous and it serves our competitors and enemies more than it serves us, as a nation.

"Everybody Owns it"

In 1055, after the Norman invasion of Britannica, the Crown, or King, held all mineral, timber, and beasts of the forest as his. After 900 years, this attitude developed into the Crown Estate, a giant real-estate and resource management consortium that generates revenue.

On the surface, a promotional video hails integrity and commercialism, with surplus revenues going towards schools. However, like any large land and resource business, and the Crown Estate is the largest, it spends most of the profits on top executives' salaries and pensions for an elite list of cronies and their prodigy.

This was a significant difference between America and the British Empire. The fact that a few Americans could go west or north to Alaska and actually remove mineral or timber wealth is very different than any other place on earth. Austria, Germany, France, Russia, and even Hawaii had all their resources firmly held by royalty. This was something Jefferson understood; the fact that free men could extract resources from land, with the understanding that tax on their efforts would go to the coffers for schools, was fundamentally different from Britain.

After the establishment of the Federal Reserve in 1912 and the preceding years of systematically weaning America away from a bimetal currency, there was less chance for smaller groups of men to create wealth from land resources.

With WW2 and the huge loans granted to large mining companies with Wall Street ties, the easy pickings of America's mineral stock was shipped to the industrial east. It was pressed into war, much of it ending up on the bottom of the sea. The American people were left with a national debt that must grow, by its very nature, until it collapses.

In Idaho, at the Triumph, the land was simply seized, not only without any compensation, but with fines imposed on the owners as well. That action was tyrannous, but far worse, it left the land managed by an underfunded office that can't possibly continue without more government funds. Where will this money come from? A successful PR campaign will continue to place the blame on the operations of the past, even though these very operations generated the revenue to buy the white marble columns and floors of the State Capital.

Just like the Crown in 1055, the state has taken the resources back, by force, from private citizens. They will now have to figure out how to fund their school system with taxes. That's bad, but worse, they will need millions to manage the lands they repossessed. This is not a jobs program that could ever possibly succeed. It will run the state into debt and the various offices will turn on each other to squabble over the carrion, much like the wolves they brought in to run the cattlemen out. We are still a young nation. In the Alps, timber and minerals are managed better because they have slugged it out more than us. This is a new battle, a second battle.

At first, our government took the land from the Indians by force and gave it to settlers. Then 130 years later, the government took it back from the descendants of the settlers, and holds it today, while the very mining companies we created build huge modern mines in Mongolia, Africa, India and Mexico, taking jobs with them. Without cost-effective raw materials, there will be very little job development. That is painfully obvious to any hard working man with enough miles under his belt to see it. But why? That's the question: Why?

Milton sells the bunkhouse and goes south.

Milton and Vernet had grown old and tired of the long, cold Idaho winters so they decided to sell the last of the assets they held and go south. They had turned over the water company to the residents. We formed the Wooden Hill Water Works, and filed a corporate charter. The group of men I call *the hunters* quickly took control of the water company and used it as a tool to keep other people out. The last new hookups were my house and Dick Sullivan's house. The group that pushed me off the board had the largest parcels, with huge lawns and horses, and made sure no one else got on the system.

The bylaws of this group clearly stated that the sole purpose of this little two-bit water company was to provide water to every lot within the Wooden Hill subdivision. They called for a moratorium on hook-ups and that was 40 years ago.

Milton put the hotel up for sale for $7,000 and explained that the back portion of the hotel was not on the lot, but over the line onto the three neighbors behind the lot. I looked at it very hard as a purchase, but couldn't see how to make it work. It was a $7,000 pass that cost me over a hundred grand in later years and a whole lot of bad blood.

The Wooden Hill survey is off by about thirty feet, twenty-eight to be exact. All of the houses and shops, except the Atlinger's prefab that was purchased by the Collins, were there since at least 1937, and most since 1900. The main road was christened the North Star Highway in 1942 and deeded to the state of Idaho from the Triumph Mining Company with restrictions. The restrictions were simple enough; no fencing or signs in the right of way. This allowed for snow plowing, keeping the loading areas around the shops and mills clear; and no signs were allowed in the right of way because unions were trying to get in the door to stir up worker unrest. The company also retained use of all road easements, as well as mineral rights and the rights to the tailings thereon. I can't say this enough because it was so clearly written in the simplest of language, but simple language is too hard for lawyers to read. They need pages and pages to clarify simple language.

The new buyers of the hotel were two good men; one was a surveyor so his first task was to try to massage the survey data so the building he bought was on the land described in his deed. The only way to do that was to change the data on the plot in the deed.

When a survey is recorded, you begin at point A and proceed in a clockwise direction around the perimeter with angles and distances until a return to point A. If the data and angles are off some, you do not close the loop correctly. You might be off by a few inches or a few feet In Triumph, it could be off by twenty-eight feet because one side of the largest parcel was replotted three times while the mine operated from 1889 to 1957.

The Silver Crown Load, which was the main base area and main portal claim, was first patented in the winter of 1904 or so, and recorded with the state. It was then redrawn fifteen years later when they wanted a patent on the Crown Point Claim. One of the angles was changed a few degrees and this resulted in a shift of twenty-eight feet at the intersection of the Baby Ethel mill site and the Big Dipper Mill site. (Show Map)

In 1970, when the nonprofit recorded the subdivision, they never asked the parent company they bought the land from to review it. The company felt comfortable with the simple restrictions placed on the sale, and later sold the mine with all those rights to Rupert's group.

As Rupert grew more powerful on the County Commission, nobody dared to challenge the roads, but he was making new enemies in the courthouse.

In the mid '80s, a shift took place in Blaine County. The drug culture generation came of age and began to move into positions of power. The old school gals in the courthouse that came from the ranching, mining, and milling families began to find new, liberal thinking Berkeley-educated Californians on the planning board. Many came from upper middle class families that sprung from very different backgrounds. Old, established social groups, like the Grange, the Soil Conservation League, and the Sheriff's Posse began to hear opinions from new groups like the Wood River Land Trust and the Environmental Resource Center.

So imagine a weekday night at the old Blaine County courthouse with offices below held by women descended from families like Swanner, Ivie, Meyers, Cammeron, and Brown. These were church-going, hardworking families that braved a hundred Idaho winters and fire seasons of August suddenly being told what to do by a new group of outsiders with a more cosmopolitan view of the world. They really viewed the older ranching families as unsophisticated dolts and for their own good, they were going to be the new power, like it or not.

The thought of a group funded by art auctions and tax-deductible gifting that would buy land and hold it, to create open space in a county surrounded by millions of acres of federally held land, was just incomprehensible to a common sense thinking old Idaho mind. You could walk out your door almost anywhere in Blaine County and set foot onto federal or state lands that would go for a hundred miles in all directions. In fact, if you planned your route, you could probably get to Canada on public lands. So why would anyone in their right mind want to buy land and put it in a tax exempt domain? Money! When you sell large chunks of California or businesses, you get taxed at a higher rate but if you gift some of those profits to a land trust or institute, you get membership into an exclusive club of other rich guys who are new in town and don't have the time or desire to join the existing social groups. They are going to create new ones, and what starts as a friendly enough exchange will soon turn into nothing less than outright war, the new group totally conquering the existing population.

Sure, they will dust off the Ore Wagons once a year and pack the Pioneer Saloon, but the people that struggled to settle are gone. This is a natural progression that has been repeated thousands of times around the globe.

The zoning laws began to tell folks that have been there for generations that they couldn't build an additional house on the ranch for their kids when their kids grew up. So where would their kids live? How would their kids carry on the family's lifestyle? Simple, they wouldn't. They would leave, and go where there was a freedom similar to what they were used to. Leaving the existing families with parcels of land that had to be whacked up by slick developers who had played the very same game in the land they left, bringing in richer and richer men who gave more and more to the land trusts, until it became impossible for anyone but the richest of Americans to move to Blaine County.

Now don't get me wrong. Life has been good to me, and although I spent a few of my early years collecting scrap metal and dumpster diving, I am comfortable. Not Lear jet rich, not liquid rich, but I can walk into the GMC dealer and write a check for a new pickup and to me, that's rich. But where will the children live, the young families? How will they get a start on the road of life?

In just forty years, there has been a fundamental shift, a torrent of government regulation penetrating every facet of American life, taking the average family away from the church and the common sense that any farm boy develops by getting kicked in the head a time or two by a large animal. This regulation has filled hundreds of thousands of heated and cooled square feet of office space inhabited by college-educated and indebted bureaucrats. We have created a Goliath that eats everything in its path, and will subjugate all in its way. I don't think anyone can stop it. It's here like a one way tide, a rising sea that will swallow everything, so we better learn to swim.

"We just need some basic rules."

In 1950, the Housing and Urban Development office set out to help house the GI's and their families. The government developed minimum standards for stick-frame construction. Now we all know what stick-frame construction is, but in the Old Country, they think we are nuts, idiots really. In the old country they build with stone or cement, and 500 years is not uncommon for a building. You could make a very valid argument that our lifestyle is roomier than theirs, but in 2008 it all came crashing down.

Fifty years of construction protectionism had morphed into banking and insurance protectionism, nothing more, with absolutely no protection for the taxpayers in the buildings they were paying on. *None*. When the crash came, municipal governments were expanding code control, adding more pages and base costs to builders' bottom lines, and many were adopting an international building code, written in the US and imposed on US installations around the world. These codes DO NOT protect people inside; they only protect the lien holders on the property.

The North Star tailings pond wash out.

Right after the neighbors called the EPA about the Road Department's use of our rock in the river washout, my ole pal, Billy Collins, built a pole barn for his horses. When the spring runoff came down Courier Gulch, it filled its stream path with gravel wash and that came across his land. So Billy went to Rollan Street, the father of famed Picabo Street, still a young girl on the Sun Valley race team then, and complained that Courier Gulch was his responsibility because he had the rock quarry up there. They placed two bales of straw in the little stream bed and piled some rocks behind it, diverting the flow elsewhere, anywhere, except Billy's property. The water ran down Victor Drive, around the corner, down East Fork Road, across it, and into the North Star tailings pond.

I had purchased an option on the North Star tailings pond from Bill Karst. Mr Karst had taken over as the lead officer in the nonprofit religious corporation Triumph, Inc. He had placed a price of $100,000 on the North Star tails pile. I began to clean it up because it was covered with wood remnants of the mine operations, with large nails. I piled that junk, burned it, and Wendy, April, and Chris Hastings set up a riding arena on the land. My plan was to put twelve small starter homes along the road, cap the rest of the land, and make a soccer field and a small parks building for the community.

I drew a plan, paid the $250 fee to the new Planning Department and upon review, was told by Meredith Sandler that the parks building would be considered commercial, and not allowed in a residential area.

"Are you fucking kidding me?" I ranted at Meredith. "Residential. It's a mine dump; it's as residential as an oil field."

The tails pond was designed to collect the water from the Mill operations and slowly let it evaporate off. It had an eight-inch overflow pipe that emptied onto East Fork Lane.

It was one of those very long, drawn out springs, where winter keeps hanging on and snowing into April and early May with cold mornings.

I watched the water fill the pond and was concerned about it some, but the pond had an overflow pipe that was working. It must have had a wooden box underneath the surface, but it collected water to an eight-inch steel drain pipe that was dumping onto East Fork Lane. And one of the two inhabitants of East Fork Lane was pounding a round piece of FIREWOOD into that pipe to stop the drainage.

I would walk by to check it in the morning and have to pry it out. No one would admit to doing it, so the water was building up. It still had a long way to go to wash out, but if it did, it could be a significant mess.

2. For fire protection, there shall be a minimum of 150 feet between residences on adjoining lots.

3. Wells and septic systems must be approved by Idaho South Central Health District and a copy of their approval filed with the County Planning and Zoning Administrator.

4. All utilities will be underground.

5. Any roads within this subdivision will be privately owned and maintained.

6. Fire protection shall be met by one of the following:
   A. Meeting the requirements of the uniform fire code.
   B. Providing an alternate water source within the subdivision that is acceptable to the Ketchum Rural Fire District.
   C. A payment of $2,000.00 per lot to the special county fund for the purchase of fire fighting equipment. Payment shall be due upon the issuance of building permits.

7. Lots 1, 2 and 6 are designated unbuildable due to hazards associated with mine tailings covering these lots. At such a time that adequate reclamation standards have been met and the property found safe for habitation, a conditional use permit shall be required to alter unbuildable designation.

8. Lots 3 and 4 are designated unbuildable due to environmental constraints arising from wetlands covering these lots. Lots 3 and 4 are designated unbuildable to provide undisturbed open space.

9. Lot 5 is designated unbuildable due to environmental constraints arising from wetlands covering this lot. The unbuildable designation may be changed by the Blaine County Commissioners on completion of the following requirements:
   A. A Corps of Engineers permit for wetlands alteration must be provided.
   B. Well and septic system must be approved by Idaho South Central Health District.
   C. A site specific soil study shall be performed prior to foundation design.

10. Lots 1, 2, 3, 4, and 5 may not be used for any building, structure, storage, business, or any purpose other than buffer space. Feeding and keeping livestock is prohibited on all lots within this subdivision. These restrictions may be lifted should said lots be reclaimed or deemed usable by the County Planning and Zoning Administrator. Fencing on boundaries of said lots is permitted.

11. A 20 foot wide utility easement is hereby granted centering on all interior lot lines.

12. Analysis for hazard assessment was conducted at this site. Documents relating to that analysis are filed under Instrument No. *309820* in the Blaine County Recorder's Office.

13. A copy of the notes, restrictions and conditions shall be provided to all prospective buyers.

14. Maintenance and weed control for all lots are the responsibility of the developer until the lot is sold and thereafter the responsibility of the owner of the lot.

Around the end of May that year, the warm weather arrived and several 80-degree afternoons sent the melt off the north sides of the bowls up Courier Gulch. The pond filled up and washed out, taking a few thousand yards of tailings with it and depositing them in a nice even layer all over Dick Sullivan's yard. He was furious with me, but I'm pretty sure he was the one pounding that block into that drain pipe.

Bill Karst started up my loader and scooped up all he could. I was out of town when it happened. I had gone down to Gooding to hand load a truckload of rock. I would sleep over, and load out before the desert got too hot.

Dan Tucker, Pat Murphy, and Bill Collins took that opportunity to corner Karst at a high school football game and convince him to pull my option and sell the land to them, for half of what I had offered.

The diverted path of the Courier Gulch drainage was established and they hired Gordon Williams to produce the North Star Subdivision. They promised the county that the property would remain open buffer space, and as soon as the ink dried on the plat, Dan moved his pole yard over there. The poles he was piling on the property were freshly treated bundles right out of treatment tanks, and only a hundred yards from the community well. The copper arsenate they were treated with was a carcinogen, and later removed from use as pole treatment material to be replaced with several other less dangerous treating salts. But my point, of what must I admit sounds like sour grapes, is that we, because I was part of this chain of events, did a poor job of managing our environment. Billy and Stubby could have sent the water into the remains of an old ditch that went the other way, but was damaged and needed some care. Dick and Dan could have made sure the overflow pipe was left to drain, and I could have stayed in town to watch it all unfold.

When Milton was *the Elder* in the community, he served as both priest and banker. Like a Jesuit, he was the ultimate holder of all power. And it was in his best interest that the young males of the town settle their squabbles in a fair and just manner, for the harmony of the village and the flow of payments to his coffers. We would meet on the front porch of the community center and talk. He used his Bible as his covenent. When he left, the males turned on each other, and for me at least, Triumph became a battleground. While we were squabbling over the residue, a great wind was blowing towards us from the East Coast.

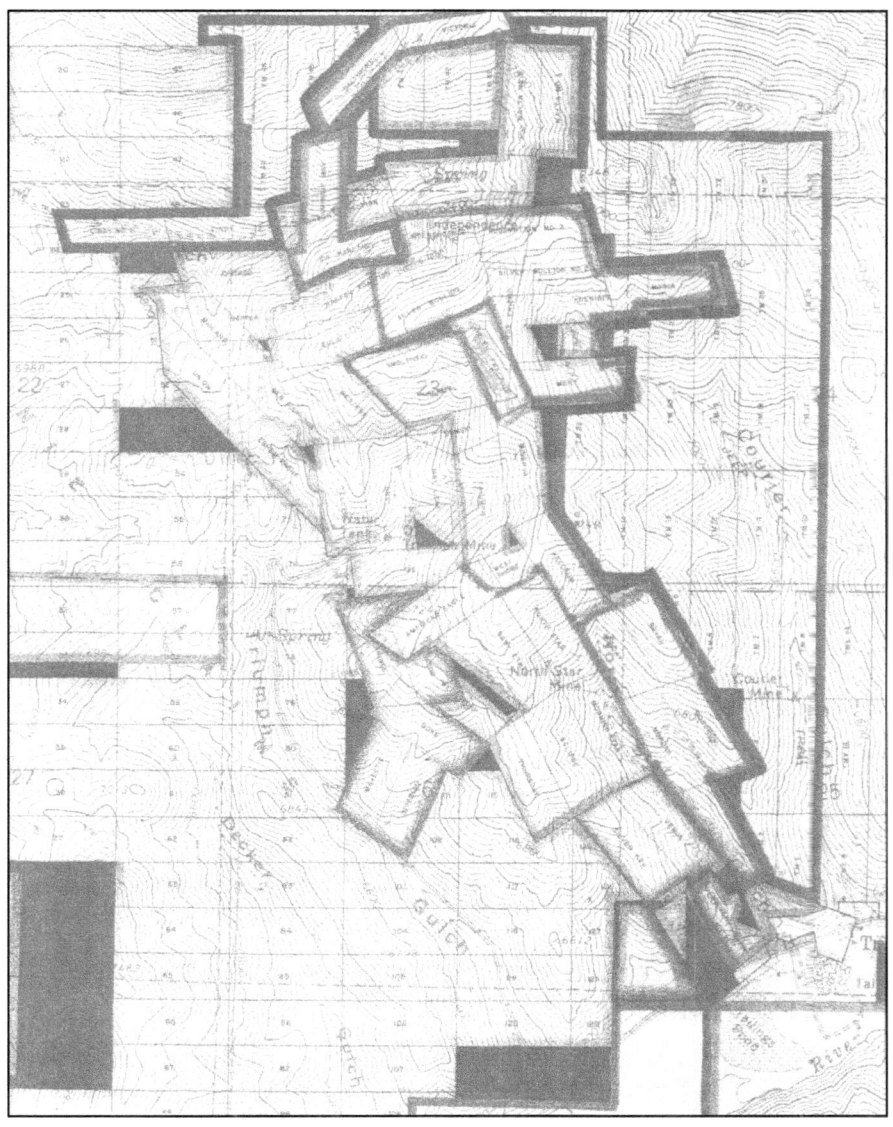

Beware of the do-gooders!

Nonprofit groups like Citizens for Smart Growth, Wood River Land Trust, The Western Watersheds Project, and the Center began to collect tax deductible donations from the wealthy people moving into Blaine County from both coasts. These people were liquid compared to the ranchers and ski bums that were settled in the valley.

Typically a respectable ski bum would be a tradesman in the summer and hone his skills on a large house for the super-rich that wanted to be left alone and stay under the radar. But as the nonprofits gained power, they began to butt horns with the older land owners.

Now in the case of Rupert, here was a man as common as the Idaho soil, who bought around 1500 acres of land, 300 in the East Fork River basin that had water. He could run some cows on it, but it was not by any stretch of the imagination *productive* land. It was high ground, and only used for a short summer pasture. He and Bonnie would buy about thirty head in spring, and sell them in late fall. He also had the controlling share in what was left of the Triumph Mine, about 850 acres of deeded land that was one of the few privately-owned mountains in Blaine County, and he had another three or four hundred acres of hilly sagebrush with the Sun Valley feeder main power line running through it.

His total investment in all this land was under $30,000. He worked at the city of Hailey garage before he ran for commissioner. He built his house from old lumber and painted his car with a brush. Most of the new money people would consider him a hick, or worse yet, a miner.

What started as a good idea...

In 1972, the federal government created the Clean Water Act, and it was needed. GE was dumping horrible crap in the Hudson, Ciby was dumping on my beach in New Jersey, Pete Seger was sailing around in the Clear Water sloop wielding the hammer of environmental law that needed to come down, and it did.

Many companies just folded up and walked away from damages. Companies like Ciba Gigi in my home state of New Jersey had been dumping crap in the ocean for years, causing cancers and still births. That waste had been getting into wells and streams. Ciba was a huge international conglomerate with a home office in Switzerland. They just shut down and walked away, leaving the US Government to try to get damages in the federal courts.

This all seemed like a good idea at the time, but I believe it backfired. When the company left, it took jobs. It left a mess and the mess was cleaned up by government agencies. Lawyers might have gotten some judgments, but those windfalls were kept by the lawyers. The people of the counties affected got little. The cities had to bring in municipal water and cap the wells.

If the federal act could have somehow provided mandatory tax deductible cleanup, the jobs would have stayed. The companies could have continued to operate, but write off the clean-up and compliance costs for, let's say, ten years, and paid no tax, provided they could show that money was being spent on cleanup. Cleanup technology would have gone bonkers, and more jobs would have been created. Instead, industry fled for Mexico, China, Canada, and India. True, these were emerging markets, and true, the chemical company scumbags only cared about the bottom line, but, in our zeal to clean up WW2-related industry, we allowed the environmental movement to kill millions of jobs, put people on unemployment rolls, and begin what can only be described as the decline of America.

Think of the absolute absurdity at the Triumph. Here was a guy with thirty cows, an old tractor, and a shack, who was presented with a bill for 4.5 million dollars for water running from ninety miles of tunnels dug under federal NRA programs in the 30s and 40s. Now the same Federal government was blaming him for the red iron sulfide coming out of the mine.

Jack Rutter told me, before he died at the age of 99, that red iron sulfide came out of the mountain in a spring when the claims were staked in 1883. That was how prospectors knew there was a massive sulfide ore body on site.

In 1980, I applied to the state of Idaho for permission to try to filter the iron out of the water and was denied, so the EPA came in like gangbusters. Our shop was demolished. My sawmill was hauled to the dump.

The BLM and Department of Lands sued each other. They sued ASARCO, because it was the parent company of the Triumph Mining Company. Asarco sued Rupert. The plug was installed against Rupert's advice at the same time the nonprofits were pushing to take all privately-held hillside property, devaluing it first by passing a draconian law that uses fire laws to restrict homes on hillsides, regardless of solar exposure. If you were rich enough to donate your hillside land to land trusts, you could come out ahead of the game. If you were local and your land was acquired by several generations of ranching, you were screwed.

Thus was the case with the Triumph Mineral Company. The only reason the nonprofits couldn't take the land was the potential liability of the tunnels and heavy metal contamination. Thus, with the stroke of a pen, every mine in the US was taken or hobbled under the guise of environmental protection. When I was at Pete Seeger's concert at Poughkeepsie, New York in support of the Clear Water sloop, I had no idea how it would hurt me twenty years later.

It's so easy to find fault with industry, especially once it grows from a medium family-owned business to a fledging stock, then a corporate golioth that has to perform for shareholders, often as the workers suffer.

I have a big problem with the hypocrisy of a nation that wants to hobble workers-- in, in fact, train a generation of children to look down on hard work and seek employment in environmental fantasy land--while the rest of the developing world takes our manufacturing base, leaving the lower classes living under a bridge. Do I sound bitter?

"You see anything, boys?"

It was a warm summer day out Cove Creek and my old friend, Tuco, had some beautiful girls from California out to his shack. Tuco was a wild kind of character—small time dealer, horse trader, and woodsman. He had a WW2 truck with a plow, and he was caretaking a 400-acre parcel of Cove Creek for an English man who bought it for resale. He sold it in later years to Steve McQueen, but on that night, after a day of watching these young ladies ride around the ranch wearing nothing but leather chaps, we sat around the campfire drinking and smoking with a few guitars. I saw a slow moving car come up the canyon, and it turned out to be the sheriff. He pulled up to the ranch gate and left his car running. It was a quarter-mile walk to our fire.

We sat in an open pasture with a small stream, while the horses were free ranging and staying close to our camp. We hid the dope, not that Sheriff Orville Drexler cared. He was not way out Cove Creek, ten miles from the highway, to bother some people for reefer or, lord knows, nudity. He took his own sweet time walking up to us across the field, his starched shirt and perfect cream-colored hat looking like he was Matt Dillon himself.

Orville was a good sheriff, and continued to get elected because he made more friends than enemies. He walked up to our fire and didn't say much. He was extra friendly to the beautiful ladies and tipped his hat like the gentleman he was.

"Ladies..." he said. "Nice night. Quiet..."

They smiled back. He had our attention.

"You boys see anything unusual round here tonight?" He looked me square in the eyes and he knew I was loaded.

"No..." I said. I wanted to say there were these girls up from California riding around naked all day and bathing in the stream, but it didn't seem appropriate.

"You see anything in the sky, or heard any cows bellowing up Muldoon Canyon?" he said in kind of an extra slow drawl.

"No. We've been outside all day and, other than a car or two headed up to the Mascot Mine, there was wasn't much going on," said Tuco. "Why? What's up?"

"Well," Orville got serious. "I've been in this country my whole life and I never saw anything like this..." He grabbed the fire poker and stirred our fire some as he stared into the glowing embers. "There were some cows killed up Muldoon Canyon about a mile from here. Their eyes, ears, and organs were removed, as if by a laser or something. Not a drop of blood or any signs of a struggle. No foot prints, tire tracks, not a damn thing to go on."

He scared the shit out of us.

"You boys keep an eye out and keep your guns handy." He motioned to Tuco's old Winchester leaning up against a chair. "If you see anything at all, contact the Sheriff's Department..." and he handed me a card.

Hell, we had no phone. We didn't even have electricity. We were all squatters, and proud of it. The only phones were back in Triumph and they were party lines. That night we all got laid, because nobody wanted to sleep alone. We were scared shitless. Real aliens, here... up East Fork. Maybe Milton was right; we were not alone and the aliens were hungry.

A few years later, Orville lost an election and took a job at the county road garage. It was very strange to see him in blue coveralls with his name on a pocket patch, but he liked his new job; "less stress," he said. He was a good man, and I found myself in a trench with him one day, installing a large culvert across East Fork Road to channel the diverted Courier Gulch water. I had offered to supply the gravel and help with my loader to get it done.

We were just two guys with shovels, in coveralls, tamping in the soil around this shiny new culvert. I asked him, straight up: "Orville..." I said, "Remember that night out Cove Creek..." I was straight as a string and looked him square in the eyes this time. "Were there really cattle mutilations out there or were you just pullin' our legs?"

He looked up from the trench, "I don't think we're alone in this world..." and he gazed up at the big blue Idaho sky. "Ever try to hold a cow down?" he smiled. "They don't like to be cut on, do you?"

That's all he said, as we finished our work and sat through a quiet lunch on the side of the road, from our identical black lunch boxes.

Slip Sliding.

A few months after April left me, I had slipped into a hole of loneliness. I had begun to drink more and smoke pot more. I sang drinking songs in my band. I was like a wounded dog out on the porch, howling at the moon. I married on the rebound, and moved back East.

The marriage was all wrong. I had left the East a long time ago, and no longer belonged there. I had to start at the bottom with a crappy construction job with a company I left in my teens, building ugly garden apartments that I hated.

One day I got a call at my mother's farm house in Ringoes, New Jersey. "Hello," I said. It was Wendy Collins.

"Carl..." she said, "April has committed suicide. She's gone."

My emotions were frozen. My first emotion was surprise; then came anger, but never a tear. I cried like a baby when I buried my dog or my horse, but when someone you knew and loved takes their own life, you feel robbed or wronged. They have taken themselves from you. It's different from when someone you love is killed in a crash or sufferers an illness. It's *very* different.

At first I blamed Wendy, and I think she blamed me. But I think April realized that she had hurt herself with years of horrible abortion brews. And when she had finally became pregnant and wanted to have a baby, when she lost it, the postpartum depression was more than she could take. She closed the garage door, ate a bottle of sleeping pills, and started up her little yellow VW Beetle. She was gone, and she will be missed by those who knew her. When you're young and in your 20s, you think you can change the world. In the end, it changes you. She thought she could change the health care industry. I thought I could change the housing industry. In reality, they have both gotten worse.

The whole home health movement was powerful and still is. But the growing government controls that we just began to see coming on, when I was younger, have now forced most Americans into a kind of slavery to an ever-expanding debt. It can't change, it won't ever, and you just need to figure out how to survive. I have gained more and more respect for the Mennonite and Quaker models. We are changing into a culture somewhere between communism and totalitarianism.

D I S C L A I M E R

COMES NOW, TRIUMPH, INC., an Idaho corporation, by and through its officers, and hereby represents to TRIUMPH MINERAL COMPANY, INC., an Idaho corporation, its assigns and successors in interest, that TRIUMPH, INC. has no right, title or interest in and to the New Tailings Dump of the Triumph Mine, which tailing dump is located south of the North Star Road and westerly of Block 2, of AMENDED WOODEN HILL SUBDIVISION, on the official plat thereof on file in the office of the County Recorder of Blaine County, Idaho

DATED this 26 day of February, 1981.

TRIUMPH, INC.,
an Idaho corporation

(SEAL)

By _____
Vice-President

ATTEST:

_____
Secretary

Tailings title.

Once the EPA came into town, I was out of business. The topsoil pit was taken by ASARCO, and they later lost it in part of their statewide lawsuit that included fines and cleanups at their mines in Northern Idaho. The ASARCO settlement gave several million dollars to the Idaho DEQ, and a yearly payment to manage the land they took from the Triumph Mineral Company, only to file bankruptcy a few years latter and that money stopped.

In 1922, the state of Idaho sold thirty-four acres of land to Federal Mining and Smelting Company with what's called a restrictive deed. The deed allows the company to put a well and run power to it. The land was what would now be called wetlands. The company was granted a right to construct a tailings pond on the land for future development. The well was dug in 1922 and a new four-inch water line was installed by blasting a ditch, and running the water to the stamp mill. The sink float mill was built in 1950, after the stamp mill burned down in 1947.

A report from the Idaho School of Mines suggested it would be safer and better for the long-term environment to rework the tails in town, both the large pond the Triumph Mining Company owns and the North Star tails that TMC retained the rights to in the sale of the town. The state just deemed them abandoned, yet they taxed me at over four hundred and fifty grand on the sale of our 850 acres.

Anyone who thinks there are property rights in this country just hasn't played the game long enough to see that they can be taken from you by a host of situations. There is a huge trend right now to steer people into city centers, urban planning, where they will become dependent on government for more and more portions of their life and weaned away from free thinking and self-dependence, just like in Russia.

"Beware of the do-gooders," Rupe would say, and I don't think he had time to read Ayn Rand. He was too busy working, raising a family and cutting firewood to keep them warm.

The Avalanche Ranch.

It was 1983, I think, and a snowy February night that had followed a long, very cold spell. I had not plowed snow in a month. I was excited, like a fireman responding to his bell.

My route was about sixteen to twenty hours long. I would load my Thermos, have a bunch of granola bars, a hundred bucks for fuel, and some extra dry gloves. I would usually have to walk up to the shop on the bench from my house at the toe of the hill. It was a good warmup and so quiet; my dogs would follow. I was like an army of one, in my mind. I spent a lot of time keeping my bucket of junk machines ready, and they usually were.

The loader fired up, the lights came on, and the snow was falling at a pretty good clip. It was around 32 and snowing big fat flakes that looked like little lanterns as they passed through the loader's work light beams.

I pulled out of my shop; the old building was straining under the snow load, as it had for years. It could hold it, but the timbers were in a permanent state of bent, like the aging workhorse that it was.

As I came down off my hill, the loader's big-mouth bucket rolled up the white carpet in front of me like an icebreaker on a solemn sea.

In 1982, East Fork was beginning to sprout houses. We had new people coming in with California money. Rupert had sold the ranch, and kept just about fifty acres. A young couple with a new baby, Brad and Joney Star, were living in the Star Ranch across from the long Avalanche Shoots on Mine Bender.

As my loader lumbered down East Fork like a yellow elephant, I sat atop it in my heated cab, the four work lights arcing a white path all around me. Fresh snow is a wonderful thing, like a bare canvas ready to record life. The snow had eased up some, but it was still coming down at a half inch per hour.

All of a sudden, in my path was something I had never seen before. I was still on East Fork Road, more than three-quarters of a mile from the base of the big mountain we called Mine Bender. The snow was covered with a nice even layer of pine needles for as far as my lights would let me see; the white blanket on the road and front yard of the Star Ranch were almost hidden by green needles. This was the most puzzling sight I'd come across. I've had all kinds of nocturnal encounters on my plow rounds: Elk, coyotes, wolverines, late night cars on the road, roll overs, and drunks. This was different. I kept rolling, did the rest of my route, and ended up at the café in Hailey for breakfast.

On the way back, I tuned up the drives that I had done already. As I rolled back up East Fork past the Star Ranch, I could see lots of big trees, some twenty inches in diameter with the whole root ball, scattered out in the field across from the avalanche shoots. Brad cut them up for firewood, but left the root balls; some are still there.

The pine needles were covered under a blanket of new snow, and I doubt anyone saw them except me.

I was just in the right place at the right time. Now think about wind moving a pine needle, okay; a leaf can catch some air and travel, so can lots of seed pods, but a pine needle is like a little spear. It has no aerodynamic characteristics. It took a huge force to push it from the face of that mountain, out across a half-mile flat to the road. By the way, it had to be ripped off its tree limb first, these were fresh green trees.

A developer got an avalanche expert to testify that that area is safe, and there are million dollar houses there now. Mine Bender is as tall as Baldy, but those shoots are a straight shot down. If the folks living in those homes could have stood on top of that mountain to get a perspective on its size, they would move. It's a very deceptive mountain; you can see it from the rear windows of the Duchin Room in the Sun Valley Lodge. The sun lights it, last thing every day as it sets.

On my first climb of it, I remember remarking, "Now I understand why they call it Mind Bender. You think you're getting near the top and it keeps going and going."

Lonely at the top.

Being the head of the Blaine County Commission had its perks. Rupe was so proud to show me the county-issued credit card he could buy lunch with every day, but the pedestal comes with some pretty nasty baggage. There are what, on the surface, appear to be hard choices, like the time he showed me why they couldn't afford to keep our ole friend Joe Danka in jail.

Joe had fallen on self-induced hard times, brought on by abuse of horse medicine and liquor. He was thrown in the county slammer for something repetitively stupid, like DUI or bad checks, but he was racking up many thousands of dollars in hospital bills to the county, so they had to put him out. When I last saw Joe, he was sleeping in the elevator of the Hailey Public Library. I gave him a sleeping bag I kept in my truck for emergencies.

Some harder games that proved to be beyond Rupe's skill set were outsmarting some of the big money coming into town, and some that had always been behind the scenes, lurking in the shadows with a much bigger agenda that any old hard scrapple cowboy could grasp— or were they?

A dedicated athlete gets into a training regime that might overwhelm the average Joe. A man who finds himself at the lower levels of the social scale, either by lot or by choice, could find the same kind of euphoric feeling at the end of a hot day on the rock pile that a runner feels after a ten mile training run. I know, because I've done both.

The Robert Redford movie, *The Castle,* is an example of this kind of physical unity and bonding. When I watch people in a busy city relate to each other, it always amazes me how people in office clothing relate to people in work clothing. This is *city thinking,* whereas in a large agricultural or wilderness area, especially where it's cold, people tend to react differently.

The beginning of control laws in Blaine County stemmed from agrarian thinking, such as selective logging of beetle back infested areas of the forest, land management for sheep or cattle; and generally, ways of using the land to produce tax revenue and permit the inhabitants of that land to grow and prosper; oh, and of course, vote.

There were side organizations such as the Blaine County Riding club, the 4-H, the Soil Conservation Office, the Sawtooth Rangers that were remnants of Roosevelt's NRA, and others that would meet and might pre-discuss a decision around a campfire prior to a courthouse meeting. But few could anticipate the changes that were coming into Blaine from Washington and New York.

In America, everything is free.

In 1963 at Socialism Central, a couple of professors, Cloward and Pivens at Columbia in Harlem, were dating. They looked around them and saw the abject poverty uptown above 75th street and the opulence on Wall Street. They had a point; there was a very clear and obvious discrepancy, and any humanitarian, a compassionate human being would feel the need for a change. A simple-minded fool, such as me, might say something like, 'I'll hire some black men on my crew and give them the same opportunity as the white men under my employ. As we might labor together side by side, out in the elements, we might form a bond, break bread together at lunch." This was not the method of change that Cloward and Pivens had in mind.

They decided that if they could get every single voting citizen living in poverty to apply for every single form of government assistance, they could crash the system. After a period of inner city anarchy, they would emerge in power, running a voting machine that would take money from the guys downtown having three martini lunches at Morton's.

I could see the point. I have been poor. I have lived in my car, played my guitar in the subway for change. I get it. Why can't we all have at least a one martini lunch at Logan's?

In 1973, when my pal Jimmy Warner and I left the East Coast to head west, his dad's business, the George Warner Tool Company at 252 Lafayette Street, New York, New York, had to close its doors because the City of New York had been successfully driven into the shitter by Cloward and Pivens.

The City of New York had major infrastructure repair and maintenance shops that required tools, fittings, you name it. The company catalog was 250 pages. The City Procurement Department heads played golf with George Senior, and made big purchases. Then when a couple of do-gooder professors pulling salaries from a state-funded school system applied their form of political chicanery to the city's social service programs, it crashed the system.

I admit, this is a street view of a big event that someone on a 50th floor might see differently. But this event was the beginning of a fire that would spread across the dry and brittle fabric of an America that was just beginning to feel the rumbles from the rickety machinery of Asia.

A message from Neptune.

It was a late September evening in Asbury Park in 1987. I was in the best shape of my life. I was a stucco contractor on the East Coast, a hard laborer with a plan. I would work the coast so I could run the boardwalk and surf as much as possible. I never asked for much. I had a diversified crew. The Philly guys were poor, white, high school drop outs that could barely read, and the New Brunswick guys were black, and actually got a better education in New Jersey so they could read better and follow orders. I, as the boss, was struggling with management, and race issues that I had never encountered before. This was on my mind as I was running my seven miles after a hard day on the scaffolds.

We were doing a job for Klinner Brothers in Long Branch, two German Jews whose father had amassed a large real-estate portfolio of garden apartments the old fashioned way. He built them, then he kept them. When he died, his two sons were forced to take over. They both took this as a step down. One had gone to Yale and received a Doctorate in English Lit or something. The other was a young man about town who competed in Air Shows with his expensive special plane.

So I'm running the Asbury Park boards, I did my run, got my mind real clear. You know, all those endorphins pushing through your veins. I finished with my kicker, I always had a good kicker, and I crossed my imaginary finish line right at the front of the Stone Pony.

Now for those of you that are not familiar with the Stone Pony, it's a dump with some really old, smelly beer coolers and a disgusting men's room. But it's the Mecca of East Coast rock and roll. The Pony is revered as a pulpit of rebellious creativity, home base for South Side Johnny, the E Street Band, the Boss, you name it. But it really did need a paint job, like all the wreckage on the Asbury Park boards.

So I finished my run. My heart's pumping like a jackhammer, and my brain is struggling with my personnel problem. One of my guys, Amp, a tall, handsome black kid, built like Hercules, very quiet, doesn't show up for work; he's in jail in New Brunswick. I need him out and on the scaffold. I have a job to do. All this is pumping through my head when fate, or god, or the universe, I don't know, sends me a message. "There were two large birds, a white seagull and a big black crow, fighting fiercely over a clam. Now, the seagull got the clam from the shoreline and flew way up in the air to drop it on the boardwalk and crack it open so he could eat it. The crow's no fool; he sees the game and he's sitting on the sign of the Stone Pony, waiting. He knows that when the seagull drops the clam, he has time to get it before the white bird can get down from the clouds. So he's on it first, then the seagull swoops in and they are going at it, screaming and clawing like a cock fight. That's when this gray pigeon, with one leg, hops on to the boards, gobbles up the contents of the clam and takes off, leaving the black bird and white bird fighting over an empty shell." That's it, that's the message, and I got it clear as a bell. We, as a nation, are fighting over an empty shell. We have been played. Is the game over?

Go deep.

Most of the mines in Blaine County are not very deep by mining standards. The Triumph is only 800 feet below the main portaland; that's nothing. The Queen of the Hills in Belleview is less. On a recent trip to the Alps, I went through tunnels that went for miles, right through mountains that held national boundaries on their peaks. I saw several new tunnels containing highways, not trains, boring through—connecting valleys so separated for centuries, as to have different languages on each side of the hill. In central Idaho, there are mines that go down 10,000 feet and are producing.

Blaine County developers and appointed officials in general, chose to create a bureaucracy that locked the gate at Timberman Hill.

In the '70s and '80s, everyone was still using a lot of whatever poison they grouped up in, coke being the upper classes with bucks, reefer being the middle spreading from the $25 bag buyers like me, to the more refined and dignified Hawaiian red bud users. Like Bob Dylan said, "I started out on Burgundy but soon hit the harder stuff."

The band and I, "Those incredible flying saucers," got to play all the big dances and balls, political conventions, weddings. I got to see people at their best and their worst. When you're up on stage with a thousand pairs of eyes on you, you get to see them too. It's an amazing experience that most people don't get to feel and I'm thankful I had those years, but they are in my rear view now.

There have been some very pretty, hot women on the city council, and the party would move around, like Rome in later years. Politics in Blaine was a party, but for me, I saw it as petty college fraternity that, between sets of beer pong, made more degrading demands on the new guy, or the old guys that saw through their game.

Who's running the show?

There were power-hungry people who by setting the stage of a master plan, stood to make big bucks. It was a variant on the classic railroad real-estate profit model. First you build a railroad, or a highway, or just an exit off a highway. Then you whack up the land around it and develop it. Well, the Blaine County Airport was on the chopping block to fall into that hustle.

First, you put all the commercial stuff there and then kill existing business up and down the highway by passing a *non-conforming use law* that basically says, "You're an existing business and we want you to die and go away."

This was the case imposed on Scott Boots, Dean Tire, Stan Johnson, and North Fork store. They were all little businesses that were locally owned by good, honest, hard-working people. They were told they couldn't modernize, or expand or change use. They were placed in limbo where their biggest asset, their building, was frozen. It wasn't condemned or taken, but it was sentenced to death by a bunch of stoners and cokeheads with the power of a planning department, staffed with new people that forced their little plan on the older locals.

Rupert hated this and saw right through it. Not only was it stealing, but it was a bad plan, because now you had to travel ten miles from one end of the county to the other to buy goods; and it stopped competition for some of the bigger merchants that were well entrenched. Most importantly to him, it put his company, Triumph Mineral, in real trouble.

When I first bought the Sink Float mill site in Triumph from Milton Harr for $7,000 dollars, Triumph was zoned Transitional Agriculture. Flat Top Sheep Company was still paying a yearly grazing fee to Triumph Mineral, and Harold Knight was running cows down in the flats below the mine. Triumph Mineral was regularly courted by geologists looking to process the tailings for the gold, and multinational mining companies were sniffing around East Fork to re-open old mines that shut down after the war.

The new non-conforming use laws skillfully killed any chance of mines opening by adding a simple clause that read: *Any business that discontinues operation for 12 months must reapply for a new conditional use permit.*

That kills small mines that sometimes lay locked for twenty or thirty-year periods, due to market demand. That kills sawmills that could find themselves shut because of a building recession or a forest fire. Raw materials don't go bad in the earth or in the forest, so a clause like this is a death sentence.

When you encourage small business, you build community. If the sawmill's lumber is a little more, you still might buy it because the owners have kids on your kid's ball team, or they're in your church or club. But when you begin to form clubs that want to close business because you think you're saving the planet, or you don't eat meat, or you hate cars, or chairlifts, or whatever, you begin to lay the framework for a dying town—or at least a very different town, a town where the children grow up and leave.

The race was on to move the Hailey Airport. The thirty-five-year argument would begin by cramming any kind of affordable housing into Woodside, a five-mile stretch of land to the east of the runway. Then came some studies about the dangers of flying over towns, complaints about noise, blah, blah, blah.

But what was really happening was a small group of "behind the curtain scumbags" were salivating over the money they would make from the acreage the old airport was sitting on, and the new acreage the proposed new airport was moving to.

There were two locations in the running, and anybody who could feel the wind blow would know they were both lousy and dangerous. They would hurt the tourist trade, because flights often would not land due to high winter winds. If you want to gauge the brunt of winter weather on an area, go look at the snow plows at the Highway Department's garage. The Camus Prairie, one of the prime relocation sites, was loaded for bear when it came to snow plows. You might as well land on a rolling aircraft carrier at sea than on the Camus Prairie on a snowy, windy day, of which there are many.

Rupert was on the airport committee, and he got the feeling a few of the parties at the table were up to no good and I think he was right. It took forty years, and millions of dollars in wasted, pocket lining engineering studies, for the county to finally decide to leave the damn airport alone and fix up and maintain what they had. Technology played a role here by introducing new flight equipment, but it was more about politics, insurance, and government regulation than common sense. The position Rupert took with the committee was one of farm boy, can-do, logic. He made some enemies, and the Triumph mine, one of the largest parcels of deeded land in the county, was under attack from the do-gooders.

I love *Cats*.

Rupert and Bonnie came to New York! By 1988, the EPA had a stranglehold on the 859 acres of the Triumph Mine. The Clean Water Act was a hammer that fell wherever it wanted. Mine discharge was treated like wastewater coming from a chemical plant, even though it was just drainage from the earth.

The Idaho Department of Lands battled it out with the Regional EPA office and entered into a contract with ASARCO (The American Smelting and Refining Company), started by Meyer Guggenheim 130 years earlier. It was determined that because ASARCO had morphed from the Philadelphia Company to the Philadelphia Mining and Smelting Company, to Federal Mining and Smelting, to Triumph Mining, to ASARCO, and they had deep pockets to attack, they would be responsible for the estimated 12 million dollars in cleanup costs.

ASARCO and Lands (IDEQ) determined that Rupert, who was previously one of their 15 dollar per hour laborers, and was now the proud owner of the mine, was responsible for half of that bill. They sent him a letter informing him that he needed to pony up 4.7 million dollars, and he could make the check payable to ASARCO. At the court hearing he announced, at the age of 80, "I could whip any one of you pasty face bastards."

But the jackals had the old lion cornered. I want to clarify an observation that I made about this process. The actual work, the moving of the earth, was done by a low bid contract by a company out of Missoula for about 250 grand. ASARCO put in the plug at around 500 grand, the rest of the monies went to lawyers, political offices, public meetings, and engineering studies up the yin yang. It was a total scam, a bridge to nowhere, a shame.

A report from the Idaho School of Mines recommended that the gold be recovered from the tailings to pay for the work, but it was easier to just take the fiat currency settlement money and sweep everything under the carpet for another day.

Maybe they did me a favor. A few years later, I was remodeling officer's quarters at Dover Air Force base during the first Gulf War, watching the same federal money spigot turned wide open and running. We had an armed contracting officer watching our every move, and I commented to him about China versus the US military. His comment was that they will never catch up to us because we spend thirteen times the amount on our military.

That day I was paying a man thirty dollars per hour to paint a young, strong air force man's room. In China, they paint their own room. I've seen how the federal government wastes time and money and we are so screwed. Around the 11th century, give or take a few hundred years, the Mongols rode over Euorpe. One reason they could do so, was the easily available minerals for weaponry near the surface at Oyo Togo. China now controls much of the mineral wealth of the emerging world. Each year, they have a national award show like our Oscars for mining executives. We are so screwed.

I had already left Triumph and moved to Philadelphia, where I started a coatings company and soon was doing very well, with respectable public school and military contracts. That year I bought several new trucks and a Black Cadillac with red leather interior. I was working like a madman and trying to make up for what I thought was a lot of wasted time in Idaho. But to be fair, I had five properties in Triumph that were paid for and sending me rents, so Idaho was still putting food on my table.

I couldn't stand being in Triumph for *the cleanup*. It was just too painful. They tore down my shop and sawmill, and hauled it all to the dump. The neighbors picked over our steel like vultures, taking old mine cars, bull wheels, and other mining junk that was part of a dying history. It was gone and I couldn't dwell on it, so I sent Rupert and Bonnie an invitation to come to the Big Apple. To my surprise, they came, and we went to see *Cats*.

I've always loved *Cats*. I know sophisticated theatergoers make fun of it. It isn't *Camelot*, or *Rent*, but it's got a great soundtrack; and as the music pulls your spirit up at the crescendo, the old cat ascends to heaven in a giant tire.

"He's going to heaven in a loader tire..." said Rupe.

For a couple of guys that spent a lot of cold, dark early mornings pushing snow in big rubber-tired loaders, it had a special meaning. I'll always cherish that visit.

My marriage in Philadelphia didn't work out. When Bill Clinton got into the White House, he chopped the military budget and turned the spigot off. Many contractors went bankrupt. Suddenly, nothing was passing muster. The tasks were the same, they just found reasons not to pay. It became clear after several months of bullshit that we were going to get screwed by our Uncle Sam.

I took my big truck and trailer down to the base while my pass was still valid and loaded up about ten grand of my materials, sold my shop in K&A (Kensington and Allegheny) in Philly and headed to Nashville with a brown paper bag of cash. I was starting over again at the bottom, with trucks and tools.

I married my old friend Lori Evans from the Waylon days, and she has put up with me and supported my creative side. I made a small fortune in an area of Nashville called Edgehill.

Edgehill was a black part of town that butted up to Music Row and was close to all the colleges. Most southern whites wouldn't live there, but I saw it as an opportunity and quickly thrived. I knew the drug culture from my years at the bottom of the ladder, and saw the houses that the dealers owned and knew the houses that the users lived in.

The hardest users lived in a house that was owned by grandma. Grandma would get a break on taxes, utilities, and there were programs to repair the house, install a new roof, cut out dangerous trees, and provide meals on wheels. Most interesting to me, around Election Day the church bus would send young kids by to wash windows, rake the yards, you name it, and then pick grandma up and take her to the voting booth.

I had a map in my office with the traffic between the dealers and users, in colors. Dealers red, users black, properties to acquire in blue, within a few years. I joined the Masons, had friends in many city departments that treated me fairly, and bought and sold over fifty properties. I became well respected, and had money in the bank.

I had made friends with a Connecticut Yankee named Ira Blonder who was very active in Music Row real estate. Ira and I hit it off and he started bringing me bigger deals. The first one was a small apartment project owned by a man named Joel Gordon.

Joel started out on the bottom rung of the real-estate business. He rented apartments in *the hood* to federally managed programs that place felons into housing when they come out. His money comes straight to him like Section 8. The ex-cons are supposed to go out, find work, and pay a small portion of the rent. However, it's an unspoken arrangement that they will never pay rent. In return, the owner never shows up to do any repairs until Codes press it.

Codes and police don't even want to go there, so the land becomes an island of crime in the middle of a black neighborhood that houses a bunch of bullies who pull everybody down.

I bought this little shit hole, 8 apartments composed of two long, one-story buildings, for 160 grand and did what's called a *horizontal property regime*. That was a process dreamed up after 9/11 to take apartment buildings and turn them into condos.

I renamed the place St. Augustine Court. That was my backhanded joke in the heart of a Southern Baptists controlled section of the hood.

The place is drug dealer central. As we began to strip the party walls between the baths and kitchens, we would find the dope, or what was left of it. Things like empty vials, crack pipes, and in one unit, we even found a poor emaciated pit bull. We called the pound.

The drug dealers had a simple system. They'd get the little kids, like six and eight- year- olds on their bikes to play lookout. They'd keep the dope in one house, up the street. They'd take the money at another. It wasn't hard to figure this out when you're putting on a new roof and can see everything.

If I was going to make any money on this project, I had to get these drug punks off the street. It was war, and after a few bricks through my windows, I won.

I got a call from a Nashville Police detective that they had picked up the two brothers that were the main dealers and were putting them away for a while. Their house was in their mother's name, but there was some pressure they could put on her.

We sold those units and made about 600 grand, with total support from Codes, the city and the Police Department. But not one unit went to single, black women, even though there were programs that made it so simple to get in. There was a ten thousand dollar transportation grant, first-time buyer incentives; monthly payment on these units were low and they were nice now, all new plumbing, wiring, central heat and air, off street parking, tiled kitchen and bath, new cabinets and appliances. But once the manager for Rascal Flats, a popular country band at the time, bought one for his road crew, then they were cool, and the rest sold like hotcakes. I had impressed my banker, who has backed me ever since.

The next deal was exponentially bigger. Vanderbilt University is the crown jewel of Nashville. It has a multi-billion dollar endowment, multiple research projects with the medical, aeronautic, and nuclear energy industries. They appointed a new dean who, among other things, was divesting any property held outside of the perimeter of 18th Avenue and West End.

At the time, school properties were going up, way up, within that perimeter. They needed parking, they always need more parking, and Ira Blonder pulled me into a three-way 1031 Exchange.

One party owned a lot behind Waylon's old office on 17th with a house on it. Vandy had a nice brick and stone apartment building called *The Hilltop* at the top of 18th, in a high-end neighborhood with old homes belonging to professors and ex-grads who wanted to stick around the campus. The building was run down; it had an old boiler in the basement, which was leaking along with the radiators and pipes that connected to it. The walls were plaster and when the leaks rotted out the ceiling, the maintenance crew just covered the hole with a piece of painted plywood and some screws. The hospital had a program for hardcore addicts coming down with methadone, and they were housing them in this building, along with some really scary hoarders that were living like rats in their nests of crap.

The building had once been a grand lady, with a thirty-inch stone walled basement that had a back wall coming out on grade with full windows. "The Hilltop" also had a 3,000 square-foot space filled with junk and leaky pipes, a boiler that was incorrectly plumbed and running all the time because some Goober had two circulating pumps opposing each other, and a utility bill of almost $6,000 a month in winter.

I got this building for 650 grand, put 10% down and put about 500 grand into it. I ran all the nut jobs out, got rid of the boiler, and had a really nice office, woodshop, and game room with a pool table.

The building was earning me about 150 grand a year and I was hanging out downstairs and doing oil painting again, after 40 years. I thought I would retire like this. The building was a cash cow and I called it a *graduate house.* I didn't care what color you were, as long as you were a Vandy grad student, you were in. I had great kids, and in some cases, foreign doctors doing a two or three-year fellowship.

I loved The Hilltop building, and I loved being around those smart kids. I would get them to shoot pool with me in the game room every chance I could and learn about their goals and aspirations. I was going to be the old man down in my shop. I had other properties and land up at the lake out of town. Life was almost perfect. I even bought a Volvo. That's when I decided to go to Sun Valley to go skiing.

Wow! How Ketchum had changed.

I walked into the Starbucks on Main Street in Ketchum, Idaho to get my morning Joe. Years earlier I had sprayed those brick walls with a clear sealer, working for minimum wage. I thought about that stuff in my lungs, and all the other lousy jobs I did so I could finally afford to come to Sun Valley as a guest and have this cup of coffee.

I thought of all the hard times hauling anything I could get my hands on to buy groceries and pay my little mortgage to Milton. I hauled rock from the desert, off the top of Stubby's peak, brick from the Arco school, and firewood scraps from the mill in Fairfield when it was 20 below, and I had no heat in that 6x6 GI truck. I froze. I starved. I lost everything at least twice and had to look for food in the Triple's Grocery store's trash bin to feed my dog, me, and my chickens.

I had made it, I thought. Much of it was due to Lori Evans, my wife and buddy who supported me in my dreams. We met in 1976 when I worked for Waylon Jennings. No matter how crazy you think you might be, *The Outlaws* were truly out there. And if there ever was a box, they were not in it.

All this was flowing through my noodle when I turned the page of the Idaho Mountain Express to the classifieds, right there for sale is the Triumph Mine, listed for

$760,000 bucks, right there in black and white. *No matter how hard I try to get out, it's calling me back in...*

I had a pretty good savings account then, and I went back to the hotel and told Lori that I wanted to buy the mine. I was still carrying paper on four parcels in Triumph, and with a few bumps, they were earning. The young architect that had bought my big barn building tore it all down and was building a mansion. He got in way over his head and lost it all, eventually, after stealing all the parts of the Triumph compressors for his house. The other building I was carrying would go into foreclosure, too, when the couple divorced, saddled with hospital debt.

It's hard to make an honest living in Blaine County. In fact, it's very hard. After forty-two years here, I get it. It's all bullshit, the rules, the programs, they are all designed to keep people out. Nobody except those that have funds from some other source can make it here. It's like a training ground, a boot camp for survival. They say "New York, if you can make it there...," but believe me, I worked the I-95 Corridor. Blaine County is hell and heaven rolled into a big swirling cloud. The result is the best ski mountain in the world with very few people on it, and that's the way everyone there, myself included, wants it.

Lets make a deal.

I called my friend Judy Cash. Judy was a smart, old school real-estate agent. I had not seen her for about ten years. She was still a sharp looking gal, and when I told her I wanted to buy the mine, she told me to forget it.

"Rupert is too difficult to work with," she said. "He wants a five thousand dollar non-refundable fee just to sit down and talk."

"Here is the five thousand," I said. "Get a signed agreement of sale right away."

Rupert's real estate agent was from the firm that Betty Laverty, a partner in the mine, was with before she passed. There were ten partners all together. Some were dead, some were still living and in their nineties. Time had caught up with all my old heroes, and it's now on my ass, too.

What Rupert was really selling was 100% of the shares in the Triumph Mineral Company. The company had assets, 52 patented claims totaling 859 acres chopped up into 14 tax parcels that have been listed since 1883, three roads, also plotted in the 1880s, dozens of easements on the surface and layered under the ground from one tax parcel to another at various levels, down to 800 feet below the main portal.

I worked with the Getty Mining division for three years, and felt confident I should throw everything I had at this deal. I knew how much silver was there. I knew how much gold was in the tailings. I knew about the water and the tram easements. I was so convinced about the value of the Triumph that I knew I could sell it. That's what it takes 99% of the time. You have to believe in what you're selling to sell it, that's sales 101. I hadn't been this excited about a purchase since my first car. I held a signed Agreement of Sale with a signature on the bottom I had seen many times in my life, on numerous handwritten contacts for rock, dirt, and scrap iron. I headed up East Fork Road to *the ranch*. Rupert's ranch was a historical western icon that was built entirely from salvaged materials carried down from the Triumph. The sides of the barn were covered with rusty old hardware and mining tools.

Many times through the years, some big city camera guy would show up with three or four hot models and do a western clothing or Wrangler photo shoot in the yard. The first door you pass from the garage begins to tell the story. They say your front door should make a statement. Well, the carport door had a pulley attached to a 10-pound window weight that held it shut to the late afternoon wind that blows down East Fork. Then comes the wind power research center. Rupe loved to make little windmill things in his welding shop. He had a dozen of them and they were spinning in the warm, late Idaho afternoon. Then there was the red door to the house. It had a bunch of coats of paint on its cracked and peeling surface. It was NEVER locked, except maybe Rodeo Weekend, because East Fork history shows that there have been unscrupulous acts perpetrated when everyone is at the Hailey Rodeo.

I knocked twice and went in.

"Hello…" I said, like I had never left. "Is there any coffee left in the pot?" I was boiling with excitement as the old man, now frail but still with that great glint in his eye, smiled when he saw me. I gave him a bear hug.

"How ya holding up?" I said.

"Been better…" he said. "I can't see. No matter how much you plan for old age," he continued, "you can't plan for blindness."

He had fallen victim to a botched eye surgery and lost vision in one eye. He could see from the other with a handheld magnifying glass.

"How have you been?" he said. "Are you married?"

He always loved to rib me. He had suffered through my failures in love, and taken in my horse for me when I had to leave the county to find work to keep my sanity. He threatened to kill me a few times, including once about ten years earlier when I got him to sell me an option to buy his 87% of the shares for $35 each. Thank god that didn't happen, I would have been broke again. He realized after he signed that he had made a mistake and wanted out. I forced him to reimburse me $1,000 for the airplane ticket and a copy machine I'd bought for the Triumph office, to make the deal. He said he was going to put a hit out on me and I took that as a racial slur. Ha, it was a riot in hindsight.

"What brings you back here?" he said.

"I'm buying some property up East Fork…" I wanted to drag this moment out for all it was worth.

"Oh," he said, "where is it?"

I pulled out the signed agreement of sale and laid it on the kitchen table. He had to get his magnifying glass out.

"Look at that signature..." I said, as I tapped the paper with my finger.

He was a bit shocked. We had some coffee and ginger snaps.

By 2006, I had bought and sold almost 100 parcels of land, lake lots, Triumph lots with homes, lots up East Fork, apartments in Philly, and a machine shop. I sold and carried paper, bought from trusts, disgruntled partners, slum lords, and little old ladies in nursing homes on their last legs. I had been kicked and scratched before, and thought I could handle this deal. I had a million bucks in equity in the hilltop building, and about 250 grand in the bank. I had another 100 grand of credit on Visa and MasterCard, and a good boat. What could possibly go wrong?

Take my stock, please.

When Rupert took over the Triumph Mine in 1969, he took on partners. He and his brother, Buss, controlled about 75% of the 10,000 shares of stock issued in a C corporation they called Triumph Mineral Company. This company raised 260,000 dollars to purchase all the holdings of the Triumph Mining Company, accomplished in a very clear chain of simple language title from The Philadelphia Company in 1883, to Philadelphia Mining and Smelting Co., to Federal Mining and Smelting, to the Triumph Mining Co., then to Triumph Mineral.

The company retained all rights to tailings, mineral rights to the land in what Milton called the Wooden Hills Sub, limited rights to the 1000 unpatented acres and rights and restrictions to the portion of East Fork Road that goes through Triumph, as well as several tramway easements on the surface of the 52 patented claims.

There was also a more recent agreement with First Light Last Rock Mining Company, aka, Stubby's Rock Quarry, for 50 cents per ton, to drive over the claims to get there.

These assets were taxed by the state of Idaho at a corporate rate. The mine was NOT abandoned, as some groups claimed. It needed every little revenue stream to cover its taxes and stay afloat.

It was not until the first few months of trying to close this deal that I began to understand the tax mess that I had gotten into. It's almost too hard to explain, but I will try to keep it simple.

The stock, 10,000 shares, had an initial cost (the Basis) of $260,000 in 1967. I paid $750,000 for that stock in 2006. If I sold it for a million, you would think I would pay tax on the difference between the $750,000 and the $1,000,000. Right? Wrong!

I would have to pay tax on the difference between $260,000 and $1,000,000 and that tax would be 34% federal corporate, 21% personal cap gains, and 7% state of Idaho. So the tax on the $750,000 sale at a million would be 62% plus a 6% sales commission, or 68% of $750,000-$260,000 or $306,000 in taxes. Half my $750k that I put in was gone the day I closed, but I didn't know it.

Then, we began to spend money to find investors and a buyer, which ran up to almost 200 grand. I went to New York several times, the Brownfields convention in Chicago, out on the Navy Pier, The Javits Center, and the EPA mine-scarred offices in Virginia. I went to Vegas and Atlanta. I met some really big players, and worked my phones day after day. I had everything in, everything. I had to pull this off; my wife was with me as always, but I could tell it was really stressing her. I got to talk to an impressive list of brokers and executives from companies like Corcoran NY, Blackstone NY, Jones Lang LaSalle Atlanta and Chicago, Met Life Real Estate Division NY, Southern Land—I forget the Vegas guys; but these were all companies with long arms—oh, and we were talking to InterWest and Fortam too.

It took almost a year for Rupert to close. Some of his partners were dead by then, and members of the estates had to sign off. I talked to a longtime friend whose name I will not mention, who was a lawyer and I thought would be helpful. He had a completely different opinion of who I was, and what this deal was worth.

Then I took on a pair of crazy New York guys that I actually got along with pretty well; everybody else hated them. Go figure. We would fight and scream and threaten to kill each other. It was great fun to me, and that made them real nervous.

One time, they threatened to break my knee and I sent them a formal letter requesting that it be my left knee because it was giving me a lot of pain already and a replacement might be in order; they shut up for a while.

The Triumph survey was a mess because the residents tinkered with it. They put up fences on property they

161

didn't own, and after years of this, they had made such a mess that it was easier to massage the survey to meet their needs than correct the fencing. The result was that they moved the road to the mine and almost closed it off, that of course being a convenient side bar.

I grabbed my ole pal Alton Stone, Stoney from Stowe. Stoney was the smartest environmental guy I knew. When Alton Stone and I got to town, his advice was for us to submit a formal plan to correct the roadway and this process cost me over 100 grand.

What should have been three or four thousand dollars for some Cat time and road gravel, turned into a pain in the ass, thanks to a nickel and dime neighbor whose place looks like a dump. There, I said it, *bite me*.

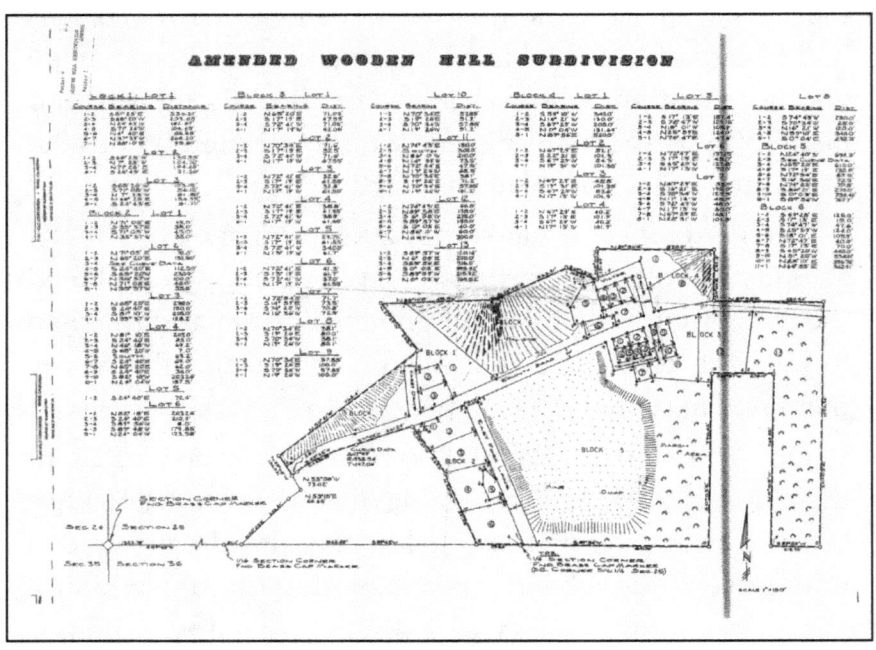

And of course in the spirit of anti-development, they accused me of re-contaminating the whole town, because remember the DEQ had done a cleanup. Now you couldn't fart out there without a complaint. If I sound bitter, it's because I am, but it's a bitter sweetness that I've learned to live with, and live comfortably.

I was now the Triumph Mineral Company's owner, with all the rights that went with the sale. I soon learned any rights can be challenged, even if they are written into a deed of agreement. There is little honor among thieves.

In 1982, Milton's daughter was the mail lady in Triumph and the mailboxes were about ten feet into the space that is now Dan Tucker's yard. We were all dirt poor, and just scraping by week to week. There was a little road to the Well House that a service truck could drive down to get at the well, and a weathered wooden rack of beat-up mailboxes that would get blasted by the snow plow when it roared up the incline coming into town.

The road through town was not paved, but covered with a yellow stone mix that the county got down near Timmerman Hill—and every spring they would come up and lay down another layer of rock and regrade the surface.

Now this may sound trivial and perhaps petty, but hang with me here, there's a lesson. No good deed goes unpunished, and I offered to let Milton's daughter move the mailboxes across the street under the loading dock of my warehouse because she had to shovel the snow around the boxes.

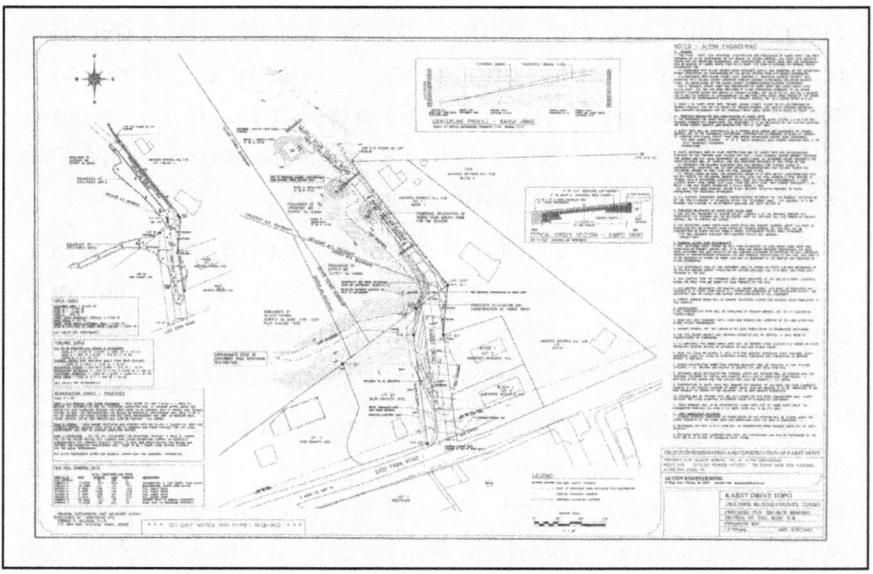

This all seemed very harmless and trivial, but then Tucker put up a fence just four feet further into the road and planted a row of trees behind it. He was on the water company board and told them that if they needed to get at the well, they could get to it across his property, no problem. The well was there since 1966 and it was an established monument that is community property.

I knew what Tucker was up to right away, because the water Board had already made a similar decision regarding the other easement to the other town well for Bill Collins, when he built a spec house that he later sold to Pat Murphy. Now the easement to the well is Pat Murphy's Drive, no problem. But on the other end of town, where the survey was in question, there was a different result.

The well, after the re-plat, was not on the lot deeded to the water company, and the mine road was not where the new plat put it either. Again this might seem trivial, but with the DEQ and EPA overtones, everything could turn into a legal fight of ridiculous proportions, with costs exceeding the cost of purchasing the whole town in 1963.

Ten years later, in 1993, in the middle of the cleanup, Tucker saw the opportunity to grab another four feet of ground. He tore down the first fence and put up a new one with another row of trees behind it; thereby absorbing the entire lot owned by the community water company and pushing East Fork Road towards my land that I offered for the mail boxes.

So he took 10 feet x 100 feet of land. Then they filed for a road shift and claimed, because the public had been driving on my land for almost twenty years now, it was a *prescriptive easement*, and I no longer had a right to it. But I was still taxed on it, and if I used it to park my truck, I could expect a call to the Sheriff's Department by a busybody bitch who knew nothing of the history of the mail boxes.

Stoney and I had to enter into the Brownsfield program with the Idaho DEQ to realign the road to the mine It took a year of bullshit engineering, visits, and storm water site work all the way up the canyon.We had to build a designated repository for the ground we removed up the North Star Gulch, reseeding with special seed, then months and months of waiting for a final sign off on our work.

All this, after the company was charged millions for a first cleanup, on land that it sold for peanuts with rights to all roads, including East Fork.

My wife and I were living on credit card debt at this point. I had burned through my 250 grand in savings and was feeling like a total sucker. Never ever give up, just pull back and wait for weakness.

The team goes to Washington.

When these federal and government agencies write their cleanup policies, they use lofty terms and broad stroke language like, *to protect the public welfare* and *for the benefit of future generations*, but there's always a money stream in there that isn't really understood until they have disarmed the Indians, and have them neatly locked into the reservation system.

The EPA has what's called a Brownsfield development program. It encourages development on mine-scarred and industrial-scarred lands by giving grants and tax incentives.

I found out about this and called the EPA in Virginia. I'm the president of the Triumph Mineral Company, I would say, and they would put me through to somebody important, like a regional supervisor of section 9 or 10. One day, I get on the line with a guy from Long Branch, New Jersey named Shahad and we start talking, hit it off, and he tells us to come to DC for a sit down.

I got Stoney and Bill to take the train down from Boston and New York, and I drove from Nashville. We set up in a local hotel, and the next morning we were in a room at the national headquarters of the EPA, sitting down with the big bosses of the Brownsfield Program. They explained to us that they had several pilot projects going in Nevada where they are taking tailings ponds and doing large solar projects on them. I got all pumped up, because I have always loved the whole solar thing. I was later enlightened as to what a scam it is from an economic point of view, but after we heard their pitch and they heard ours, it was a bromance.

They were holding a big Brownsfield conference in Motown, Detroit City, and they gave us a free booth, signage, and pencils. The government had calculated that there was over a trillion dollars in Brownsfield development real estate that was just waiting to get back into service—after its enforcement and fines ten years earlier bankrupted the American companies that had previously held the land, and forced them to pack up and move to Mexico, Canada, or just die, like the Triumph Mineral Co. was doing.

GM in Detroit was a perfect example. They built tanks, trucks, and aircraft engines at a historic rate for the war machine, and then had all the waste out in the back lots. The EPA came in with hundreds of millions in fines. A big part of Obama's bailout was the restructuring of those fines and sites to get that monkey off their back, calling it re-evaluation.

GM had lots of big old plants, like the Fisher Bodyworks, that were simply painted with lead-based paint that would cost hundreds of millions of dollars to remediate, following the laws as they were now written.

I got to see the process carried out in Triumph and I can tell you, for every dollar that is actually spent on site work, there's fifty spent by lawyers and political agencies; all being billed to the PRP (potentially responsible party). Of that one dollar spent on site, 30 cents is used for plastic soil cloths, field monitoring, soil samplings, and special seeds that won't hurt the wild seeds.

To me, the whole process was like a pack of vultures eating your family dog, sprawled dead in the yard. You loved him, and he deserves better than that.

Stoney and I went to Detroit. It's a complete shit hole that makes K&A in Philly look like a country club. There were big old '40s style offices that were abandoned downtown. There are casinos in Center City that smell like the Port Authority on Sunday morning, and then to top it off, there was a monorail with stops and stations that circled this whole mess so you got a good aerial view of it all.

If we walked two blocks from our hotel convention center complex, we were accosted by scruffy black men saying, "Hey man, you got a twenty?"

"Nigga, please, get an accordion and a monkey or something."

I had made a contact in Atlanta with a company called Jones Lang LaSalle. They have been in industrial real estate since the 1700s and were based out of London, but have offices worldwide. They saw value in what I had that I didn't and drove up from Atlanta to my office in Nashville right away. They had several potential buyers. One was a company called Southern Land, which built most of the larger skyscrapers in Atlanta on Peachtree Avenue. Another was a company called Denovo, which had just finished cleaning up a large parcel of ground in Louisiana that was owned by BP. They had a chunk of money that they had to spend in a 1031 exchange or they would be taxed.

The agent from Jones Lang arranged for these guys to meet us on the convention floor in Detroit. Stoney and I, all suited up, set up our booth in this very large room off the main convention floor. This was the third Brownsfield conference I had attended, and by now, I was seeing the same faces, but this was the first time I had a booth. A booth at a major conference, like the Jacob Javits, could cost 10 grand. The main floor of these conferences had companies that showcased their engineering expertise, like soil stabilization fabric, microbial organisms genetically engineered to eat specific chemicals, and loan sharks that got you hard money if you were a company on the ropes. Then there was AIG. Ha, what a joke in hindsight. Remember this was before the crash, and AIG was out there backing up these cleanup projects at high rates. But it's all a boondoggle of paper separation, layered into a land project; to take a whole bunch of dollars, spin them around and create an air of squeaky clean respectability to an old factory site, so it can be reused for a Home Depot or an urban mixed-use apartment site.

The Federal Government offers infrastructure incentives, like low interest loans for sewer and water line construction, loans that will be serviced by the increased density.

If a private developer goes in looking for increased density, he gets villainized. But when the Mayor's Office can call in his PR machine for the ribbon cutting, it's okay.

Detroit was like getting to see OZ, it was all bullshit. Now I saw the machine that came into Triumph and its roots. I felt like an Indian getting to go to Washington and seeing where the white man comes from.

That night Stoney and I hit the convention hotel bar and hung out with the EPA guys. This was before the wind power fields had really ramped up. Stoney and Shahad were doing some extensive bar napkin engineering of wind tower bases, and we were all hitting the Sambuca. Triumph Mineral was buying. I only had a few thousand left on one of my six maxed-out MasterCards.

Around 11, we were all loosened up. Shahad got me aside and said to me, "Carl, you have a good project and I would like to help you, but Idaho is fucked up."

He couldn't tell me why, but it did sink in and got my attention.

The next day, on the convention floor, a couple of young aggressive guys walked up to our booth and introduced themselves. Brian Pitcan and Ryan Cronk had shiny shoes, a yellow note pad and a clipboard. They were shopping for toxic properties, and already had several on that notepad. One was the large empty swampland to the west of the Delaware Memorial Bridge, in Delaware. This parcel was severely contaminated with munitions-related chemicals from DuPont's war production, and had a portion of an old shipping dock jutting out into the river. I passed it a thousand times and never thought about it. A company like DuPont would still have it on their books, and it would be identified as a toxic site that required clean up. They couldn't sell it to just anybody, because they had made the mess. It didn't matter that they made the mess for the US military war machine, just like the Triumph mine, it didn't matter that DuPont was also doing business with IG Farben, Germany's war machine, just like the Triumph Mine, and it didn't matter that almost all these companies on this sales floor, in one way or another, were doing what they were asked or forced to do, really, by the Roosevelt Administration's NRA and the War Procurement Board.

What mattered is these new EPA regulations that were initiated in the late 1980s and early 1990s essentially took the very lands from the companies that were working for Uncle Sam.

Think of it like doing business with Costco. Let's say you're a roasted tomato producer. You enter into a long-term volume supply contract with a giant company that takes 90 or 120 days to pay you, and then they end up taking you out with their own brand.

Denovo had figured out a patented way of taking over the entire PRPs burden, and layered in an AIG policy that completely indemnified the previous owner.

For this service, they got the land for next to nothing. The C Corp that held the factory site or refinery site was released, paid no corporate capital gains tax on land they probably didn't pay much for in 1930s. Remember, the capital gains of a C Corp are taxed at 34% so if you are an old corporation like the Triumph Mine, you may have paid $17,000 for the North Star claim in 1883. Actually you paid nothing, but had to show the Federal Government that you invested hard development money to receive a patent on the claim, much like the railroads. In the case of DuPont, they might have paid a few thousand dollars for this worthless, tidal swampland along the dirty Delaware in 1900, if that much. So if they sold it for, let's say, 10 million, the government would take $3,400,000 in taxes. But, when the buyer finds out how toxic it is, they come back at DuPont for the 10 mill plus damages and the IRS doesn't like to do refunds. But if an entity like Denovo steps in, they essentially launder the transaction, then they get the cap gain. So when Denovo sold a BP petroleum refinery site along I-10 to a big box mixed-use development, they had 100 million in cap gains they had to spend.

Stoney and I had a price of $25,000,000 on the site. At this point we had three offers of around 2 million, but I had put more than that into it. In the end, it would be a lot more.

Just before I got wrapped up in this deal, I had purchased another apartment building on Music Row. I always wanted a piece of Music Row in Nashville; it's the Nashville equivalent of Hollywood Boulevard or Madison Avenue.

When I worked for Waylon on the row and watched a steady stream of songwriters like Rodney Crowell, Kris Kristofferson, and Townes Van Zandt come through the office, peddling their songs and looking like homeless hippies. I decided that I was going to own a piece of Music Row someday. Up until 2004, I had homes and apartments all around it but not actually on *The Row*, as it's called.

I had a new project, an old rundown, one-story apartment called *The Danwood* that had been rented to musicians. I had to run them all out. A few tried to hold out and extort me some. I told them they could take the refrigerators, but they had to go.

The place was a total pit, leaks, trash, my usual fare. I had almost a million on the hook and another 400 grand for the remodel. It was a gut and go, tile, new AC, my usual. But this time, I was into the Triumph deal too, and it was killing me.

I was laying floor tile and talking with the head of commercial real estate for Met Life. Not only was it all wrong, I just couldn't keep getting up and down and answering my phone. My knees were killing me.

I got the first unit done, and it looked real good with a nice new kitchen. I sold it for 167 grand, but the profit was just used up to service the debt.

So finally, after a year and a half of trying, changing brokers, and being den mother to five partners who all hated each other and were trying to take the deal from me, I got a call from John Vic at Johns Lange LaSalle in Atlanta.

"Denovo wants this to happen, it will happen..." he said.

The date was set in July for a closing of September 12, 2008, the day Wall Street's foundations began to crumble.

Our buyer wanted an extension of a few days, my lawyer buddy was on the Colorado River. Alan Saturn, my Nashville attorney, gave me a tongue lashing.

"You can't do a deal like this without a lawyer, who's your lawyer? What kind of lawyer have you got?" he said, "Where is he? I'm taking over..."

I was walking up Baldy every day, on the phone to the partners in New York who were simply servicing my debt. I ended up having to sell the hilltop building to close on the mine, and I got hit with $100,000 in capital gains tax on it.

At this point, I had put up all the money, taken all the risk, piled on over 200 grand in credit card debt to move the road and make the sale. To top it all off, my lawyer buddy took off to the Grand Canyon on holiday. The New York investors were paying the interest on the note, and I was trying to sell these condos on Music Row.

I was pulled at all ends, and on Sept 14, 2008, Bear Stearns, Lehman, and AIG lost almost 90% of their value. The world was in free fall.

The buyers had a cancellation clause in their Alta Policy that even allowed them to get the 100 grand hard money back. They exercised it, pulled out and the deal was over.

I had to sign off on it. Two days later, they came back to the table for 1.7 million less and I had to take it. I had no choice.

I paid all my investors four times what they put in. I paid my lawyer buddy, who was river rafting, almost 300 grand; he waited a year and sued me.

It cost me and Lori another 130 grand to defend ourselves. We won, but all he got was a reprimand from the courts. In that deal, I learned that the courts don't work, the law is up to constant and never-ending reinterpretation and owning a corporation offers little or no protection of any kind.

Recalling a simple time.

Years ago, back when people in Triumph got along better (before the EPA, before Peekie's Olympic Gold, before Wendy Collins made herself a minister, before Dan Tucker turned the center of town into a treated pole yard and junkyard for his old used up trucks), the kids used to play on the tailings pond and the ladies would ride their horses on a simple dressage track. It was dusty, but flat, and as people drove past they could watch a fine horse go through its paces, even in winter, for seldom did the black sands hold snow.

One day, I went to a yard sale down East Fork and there was a wooden Louisville Slugger and a bucket of softballs. The sticker said five bucks. I bought it and went up the hill.

It was a warm sunny Saturday morning. Peekie, Bobba, and Patrick were playing down on the black sands with their bikes. They were 12 or 13, and I walked on down with the bat and a few balls.

"Hey..." I said, "Let's play ball."

Bobba pitched one in and I hit it out. A game started. Then one car came by and stopped and Craig got out. Then another car. Stubby got out. Then another... It was a kind of magic, spontaneous moment and we proceeded to play ball on an empty lot, on a sunny day. Pretty soon, there were several cars and we had two teams.

A few months later, when I submitted my plan to Meredith Sandler for 12 little solar starter homes, a ball field and a club house, she told me the club house was commercial.

Today, on the 4.5 acres I have left in Triumph, there are two little girls playing on my sand pile, with not even a swing set. The local residents scowl at me, as I drive by in my work clothes on my little Caterpillar skidder, like I'm the devil, evil developer, gearing up to tear the mountain down. They send me emails calling me *white trash mother fucker*. Hate is a funny thing. If left unchecked, it can fester.

I have worked very hard in my life. I remember living in my shack down by the river, and living on eggs and peanut butter, and sage grouse. I don't want to hate, and I'm tired of being villainized for wanting to build homes for people. That's what I was trained to do, but anti-development folks will always be out there. They were there when they built the Parthenon. They were there when they built Central Park and the Philadelphia Art Museum. They are part of an equation. I just try to keep a song in my heart and get up and do something,

"Try to lay a few bricks every day," Jack Rutter once told me. "Pretty soon, you'll have a house."

America builds about 40,000 homes per year, just to keep up with its normal population growth. Life happens in those homes. Life is not easy, so why do we keep making it harder for life to happen? We saddle each other with more rules, more debt, more guilt of social responsibility, more insurance, yet life still happens. Amazing isn't it?

Lead for batteries.

In 1889, the Philadelphia Company was in need of lead and zinc for batteries. Electric forklifts in factories were a giant leap forward in materials handling and electric cars were looking like a real competitor to gasoline cars.

Batteries have been around for a long time. Long before Ben Franklin attached a string to a Leyden jar, long before the Greeks discovered magnetite would point north if floated in a bowl, long even before Moses fled Egypt with the secret of the Arc of the Covenant, there were *Bagdad Batteries*, clay jars with copper stoppers and lead zinc anodes. When lemon juice was added to the jars, a chemical reaction occurred that made volts; and when linked together in series, batteries were created.

Some archeologists theorize that the ancients could use this technology for plating gold or silver onto tin or bronze.

In 1984, a man named Gordon Bird rolled into town and entered into a contract with the Triumph Mineral Co. to process the Independence tailings. He did extensive drilling and testing of all the tailings in Triumph.

Gordon was a retired chemist from Connecticut, and a very bright man. He put together a pilot plant up at the Independence, using steel wool to extract the gold and silver from the black sands. It looked pretty shabby but worked, and when he tried to enter into a long-term agreement on the Triumph tailings, he was given an accelerated royalty schedule linked to the spot price of gold.

I thought Rupert and his partners were being a little greedy here, because this guy was sticking his neck out and ready to build a plant. The neighbors in Triumph were violently against it and claimed it would be a Nevada-styled heap leaching, ruining the river and ending life on East Fork as we know it.

I visited Gordon at his plant in Blanding, Utah where he was extracting gallium from tailings. The plant was clean and very interesting. He took a giant old Worthington compressor, much like our old compressors left up at the portal, and he ran it very, very slowly in reverse. He was using a much smaller motor than it was designed for and gearing it way down by means of a gearbox, thus creating a vacuum circuit. The vacuum was linked to a series of plastic tanks and plastic pipes. This was where I lost him, but the plumbing looked fairly simple.

At the end of this rather long circuit was the end result. Gallium is a silver fluid metal much like mercury. It's used in computer chip manufacturing, all kinds of lasers, and nuclear devices. This metal turns liquid at 85 degrees Fahrenheit.

Gordon left us a lot of data on all three tailings sites. He had a massive heart attack and had to stop. By my rough calculations, with gold at 1600 per ounce and silver at 40 per ounce, there is about 65 million in heavy metals in the Triumph tailings. It's mostly in gold, because they were not processed for gold. I estimate about 18 million in silver and gold in the North Star tailings, mostly in silver, because the old stamp mill was very inefficient. So, not adding in the value for the graphite, which has seen a renewed increase in value in hydrogen batteries, there is about 80 million sitting on the surface in the tailings piles in Triumph.

One pile, on land that now belongs to The Old Dan Tucker Fence Company, is being continually capped with the hope of someday selling building lots. Think of it like letting your child play on a carpet with some nasty stuff swept under it. It was subdivided years ago, with use restrictions that were completely ignored as soon as the ink dried.

The other lower tails pile is property of Triumph Mineral Co. and part of the DEQ cleanup. They will not even let me on it and don't even take my calls. State lands will try to claim abandonment. However, when the mining claims were sold, they were there to collect the 200 grand in state tax money.

The absurd irony here for me is that a very small, low output plant, enclosed in a 50 x 100 metal building, could produce a 2-million-dollar-a-year cash flow for 40 years, and contribute revenue to the State of Idaho School fund. Reclaim the land completely and leave it for a track or horse ring. It could grow spruce trees, if the tails are amended with mulch and compost.

As part of the ASARCO settlement, the state received money to monitor the Triumph cleanup. Like any government agency, they can do no wrong. But I couldn't understand the shift in the state, away from encouraging revenue for the school system from minerals, timber, and grazing, until I discovered the activities of *The Western Watersheds Project*.

John Marvel, a Delaware architect, has built a political organization from a small office in Hailey Idaho that strikes fear in the halls of the Idaho Cattlemen's association and the State House in Boise. His group has successfully sued and won numerous cases that have changed the face of the American West. They have attacked *the Cowboy Myth* and exposed it for what it was: "a good old boy network of wealthy ranchers, herding cows and sheep on government lands and damaging the stream banks." At least that's what the mantra is, but I'm guessing the buffalo walked up to the stream bank a time or two.

Western Watersheds has a huge war chest for legal battles that they just overwhelm the state offices with, wearing them out, and infiltrating them. With this process, they have changed land use policy in the entire Rocky Mountain region.

The new trend is government control by tax-exempt nonprofits that raise revenues from suing mining, logging, and cattle companies. The revenues lost will result in raising taxes on the population.

This will have multiple impacts. First, the mining companies will pull out, taking jobs and royalty revenue with them. Second, American industry, which is already on the ropes worldwide, will not be able to even get raw materials to produce widgets. Timber will burn before it's harvested, and federal fire budgets have already skyrocketed. Food supplies will move to a smaller list of larger corporate producers, and more people will be competing for fewer jobs.

Let's look at the potential for the raw materials from Triumph. First is the gold, which would be used to service bank debt for a plant. Then we have silver, lead, zinc, cadmium, iridium, graphite, and traces of copper. The entire pile of tailing is sitting on a spring-filled wetland. In the case of the upper tails pile, the ground water is infused with the human waste and urine from the village sewer system. A fairly acidic fluid, it's like a giant super-low voltage pile of gray sludge that could make jobs and produce revenue. But that would take work, and it's easier to just sue a giant mining company like ASARCO and let the lawyers and bureaucrats pretend to be doing something. They just permanently stigmatized the property as a toxic site. In reality, it could be a small producing powerhouse, possibly even keeping some of the raw material in the county or state for use in products as simple as gold and silver jewelry, or a Sun Valley Krugerrand.

For this kind of thinking, or dreaming, I have been villainized by most of the residents of Triumph who do not own the mineral rights to the land their homes sit on. These were retained by the Triumph Mining Company in the 1963 deed to Milton's group, then conveyed to Triumph Mineral Company, my company, then sold to Denovo.

I did not sell them my rights to the lower tails pile. In '78, a judge awarded the tails on Donald Ramsey's land to Triumph Mineral Company, if they could get them off in three years.

This was a ridiculous landmark case that took something that was retained by agreement. But that is the trend, and the state will most likely try to apply this case as reason to take my claim to the Triumph tailings from me.

There were times through the ages that the mine closed for many years, only to reopen when material prices rebounded. To apply real estate law to mining is like trying to breed cats to dogs. There are basic Roman and English land laws that apply, but raw materials are a stock in trade linked to the ebbs and flows of a world market. The reason they were granted tax exemption status by the federal government since Jefferson's days is they are the beginning of the manufacturing stream. That stream flows through the back street forges to the main street shops and is often funded by Wall Street investors, creating jobs and far more taxation opportunities for the state along the way.

We have turned on those resources like a pack of rabid dogs and are wanting to tear them to shreds. Across the Pacific, the sleeping bear is not only awake, but he's already been to yoga and is at the gym benching 420.

I often wondered if the whole Cloward-Piven, socialist, environmental movements are linked at the hip and secretly funded by our communist enemies. I know Hoover thought that. It's a big picture that has fiat currency, World Bank, world power overtones. But when you add up all the cleanup sites in the Rockies that produced raw materials, and calculate all the hundreds of millions of dollar spent to close them, you might wonder why our Gross Domestic Product continues to shrink and our welfare rolls and homeless population continue to grow.

A social scientist with a doctorate in human behavior could rattle off a bunch of stats about why we are in the shitter, but when daddies have jobs and bring home paychecks, there is less chance they will fall prey to the devil's idle hands. That isn't Biblical, that's just simple common sense.

Since Gordon Bird passed, since Rupert has passed, the reclamation technology, like all technology, has improved a hundredfold. There is a convention every year in Vancouver, British Columbia, of companies trading, buying, selling, tailings reclamation systems.

Meanwhile, the Triumph site is mired in the remnants of a bitter EPA cleanup and increasing regulatory costs from the state, county and federal agencies surrounding it. Hell, even the power company pole truck doesn't want to dig for fear of a recontamination accusation.

I have a YouTube video of a pipedream project called *The Shadow of Sun Valley.* The neighbors oppose it and things have recently moved to screaming and shoving, the step before punching and vandalizing. They will stop at nothing, including accusations of recontamination, to keep me off my remaining acres.

I built a new mail box building, at my expense, and I put a little bulletin board on it. Often when I come into the shop in the morning, I see threats on it like: *There will be blood,* or *Go home, Carl.*

When I left Triumph in 1988, I was still carrying paper on five properties so I would have to come out to deal with issues. I left three large military 6 x 6 trucks up on the bench, near the main portal, and vandals took the motors and transmissions out. Triumph Mineral has been kicked, spat at, vandalized and maligned for the past 60 years, but the raw materials remain and the US dollar continues to fall in value to a barrel of oil. At some point, someone will retrieve those materials. It could be next year, in 100 years, or in a thousand years.

I have a friend, Ed Flood, who at one time lived in the house on the hill on Victor Drive between Stubby's place and what is now Kelsey's. In fact, I think at one point he owned Kelsey's house, too. Ed was a trained geologist and helped Stubby file on the rock quarry. Ed went on to become the CFO of Ivanhoe Mines. They once owned the Challenger claims at the Triumph.

Well, talking about mines remaining dormant, way out in outer Mongolia, during the time of Attila the Hun (now that's going back a while), there was a surface area on the barren tundra that had copper oxidizing in the weather. When mixed with tin, this made the war weapons the Huns liked. Spears, bronze swords, shields, and horse harnesses. About 15 years ago at a place called Oyo Togo, Ed's company, after an extensive drilling and computer modeling program, began to build one of the largest mines on the planet, with a 160-year reserve of copper, lead, silver and gold. The main elevator shaft is as big as a boxcar, and the mill is as big as a GM factory.

All that resource investment will go to factories in China. Every bar, stick, and ounce will be turned into part of their GNP while we continue to spend printed US dollars paying bureaucrats to oversee the mines they padlocked, bankrupting their owners and extending unemployment benefits to men and women sitting home watching Ricki Lake. It makes me sad and sick.

Dave Mako, the head geologist for Getty during the drilling years of the early '80s, was convinced that the land to the west of Triumph on the Annie Claims held a world class find, and the Triumph was just scratching the surface. I met with an 85-year-old mining engineer named Milton Fife for coffee. Milton started at the Triumph in 1941 at the age of 17. He asserts it was the unions that shut the mine down, not the market. He recalled union workers sleeping in groups of three and four on the graveyard shift. Both he and Rupe hated the unions. At the end of 1957, Milton told me he was working on a 70-foot face of solid silver and gold ore at the 900-foot level. If you talk to people that live near what's called the Avalanche Ranch, they will tell you that the water leaves a red iron ring and tastes lousy. Massive sulfide is indicator of an ore body.

I have had the good fortune of traveling the Alps, and they have a very different approach to resource management. They are, like it or not, ahead of us. We are no longer the greatest country in the world. True, they are mired with the same fiat currency debt problems we have and in some EU countries, like Greece, they are in much worse shape. In regards to resource management, timber, minerals, aggregate, bio mass, etc., they are way ahead of us because they have to be to survive. Every tree is used, and graded.

While skiing on Baldy, I made a comment to a friend about all the dead trees, and his response was they were leaving them to rot producing a more natural forest floor.

"Ants need to eat too," he said.

I was just a bit shocked, but the fact is, some environmental extremists take a Buddhist approach to resource management, a *do-nothing approach*. But to enforce this do-nothing method, we keep an army of bureaucrats and enforcement agents on a state, federal and county payroll. The costs from this kind of thinking are staggering because they leach into everything around us, making the cost of building a home in Blaine County five times higher than the national average.

That figure might be disputed using sales stats, but sales stats reflect a loss for most people. Very seldom do people selling a new building on spec here make a profit. They lose fortunes and end up embroiled in lawsuits with municipalities over service promises, sewer arrangements, water fees, etc.

Then there's the animal protectionism. This one I find particularly interesting because of the parallels between the wildlife and the inner-city poor.

They both are just inventory for a Cloward-Piven style agenda that expands government programs beyond revenue until the system collapses. There is a wetland that has developed around the Triumph tailings pile that was built by the busy beavers of East Fork. When I came in 1974, there was a man named Wade Gutches who would trap the beavers in the Triumph area, and at that time, the skins were purchased down in Twin Falls at the metals scrap yard. This was done with the blessing of the Water Master, who checked on the irrigation head gate that was, and still is, on the river at the end of the State School Section #10. This head gate fed a ditch that ran all the way down past the Star Ranch, and it irrigated the field that is now subdivisions.

This was the balance in place that was maintained from the turn of the century. Within a few years after Brad and Joni Star gave up their little farm, after Joni lost a baby, and the stress of that loss broke them apart, the trees up and down East Fork began to die because the ditch that fed them fell into disrepair. Donald Ramsey cared for part of it and kept a small flow of water to the tailings pond.

I always loved the pond, and would swim in it as the summer progressed and the water warmed up. It had large trout that would get trapped in there and congregate at the eastern end in the grasses. Geese and occasionally Trumpeter swans would land and stay a while.

When the EPA came in and told Rupert how it was going to be, part of the pitch was that the shape of the pond was concave and they were going to make it convex; so it would no longer hold water. This explanation was not only bullshit on the surface, it contaminated the resource, i.e. the tailings, with the lower dump run rock that was on the bench in front of my shop.

To demonstrate, take two large pie pans; let's say 16-inch pizza pans. Place them on a table and in the center of each pan, place two cups of flour or corn meal in a little pile shaped like a volcano with a crater on top. Now take a cup of water and pour it in the crater on top in one pan. In the other, pour it in the pan around the volcano; walk away and come back tomorrow. Both piles will be saturated, one having wicked the fluid up from its base, and the other from the crater on top.

The explanation for capping the tailings was bad science and any Eagle Scout could see that.

Rupert was broken by these younger men and too distressed to fight, but now twenty years later, a generation, the beaver have moved in all around the pile and it is wicking water up from the wetlands it sits on. This was predicted in a 1987 report produced at the Idaho

School of Mines (an institution that is now gone), and put together by Professor Bis Pessic and Bill Rember, PhD.

Bill is now in his mid '70s, but he grew up in Triumph and as a young boy, he told me he retrieved enough gold from the mill tails to buy a bicycle. They advised that the state process the tailings for the metal's value and then pump the tails back into the tunnels at the Plummer Tunnel entrance, thus plugging the tunnels from far above the main portal.

Now to be fair, this plan would have its problems too. It would take longer and be more disruptive to the community, who were all stressed out and angry, and still are. And at that time, gold was at $265 per ounce.

Donna Rose was a powerful and pretty woman who went all the way to Washington to protect her investment. She had purchased Donald Ramsey's place and he retired to a farm in Missouri. Donald was one of the best neighbors I ever had. If he had a problem, he came and talked about it calmly and peacefully. His fencing on East Fork reflected the real property lines. As soon as he left, things began to change and a land grab started.

Metals Research Corp.

Down in Twin Falls, at the end of Kimberly Road, there is a small, brown metal building with some old mining cars in the front yard. A simple sign *Metals Research Corp.* is above the door. About ten workers, all wearing sidearms, attend to an immaculate shop that looks much like a brewery. Inside there are several 1,000-gallon stainless steel vessels in a row, linked with pipes and pumps. This is second generation technology, far surpassing the heap leaching of the 70s.

This company was started in a little house across the street that is now gone, by a man named Charles Wolchak. His son has taken it to a whole new level. He gets tailings concentrate shipped to him from all over the world to Kimberly, a dairy town.

The material is very heavy and comes in steel containers about 2 x 4 x 3. He runs the sand-like material though his still and gets 99.9999% pure gold out the other end.

He then takes the cleaned, or processed, material, and ships it back to Mexico, India, and Canada.

Not one of his clients is in America because he and his father learned the hard way that mining in America has become a political nightmare. And this brings me around to the question: Why?

Who most benefits if we don't have access to raw materials? Who most benefits if we continue to reject a bimetal-based currency? Who most benefits if we have a generation so far removed from the age-old sciences of metallurgy and mineralogy?

Now, I'm just a rock hound and a cat skinner, but the angry mobs that have kicked my doors in and slandered me as a demon developer are, for the most part, out of work, retired (living on a pension), or working at a government job. Their children have grown up and left because there are few opportunities in Blaine County. This *grow up and leave* statistic is debatable because many children, since Ulysses, travel to other lands in search of fame and fortune. The few that do return to Blaine County must first make a fortune elsewhere to live here, or they will be destined to shine the rich man's shoes. And, there are rich men with shoes to shine everywhere, so I admit, my case could be flawed. If a very small pilot plant with state support would be allowed, even if it was just a simple lab table and pilot research program with college interns, a job-producing business could create tax revenue for the school system and a 30 or 40-year business whose core products (silver, gold, lead, and zinc) will continue to climb in value. So the slower and smaller a company could process this material, the better it could serve the state and community.

If our dollar continues on its path, and all indications show it will, gold and silver will continue to climb, hitting $3,000 an ounce in ten years. Machinery and plant equipment placed in service and cared for will only earn more as its costs are paid down. The little company's revenues will climb. The fly in the ointment will be environmental groups and ne'er-do-well NIMBYs that pile on frivolous suits to stop it.

I know many have the opinion that I'm on a fool's errand. If I die or get stopped in this quest eventually, state-sponsored programs will claim that Triumph Mineral has abandoned this land, and or been negligent in its care. A state-funded resource recovery program (funded by fiat backed federal debt) will process the sands; the gold and silver will disappear into the ethos of time, likely finding its way to a private vault in a politician's home. This has been the problem with gold since the beginning of time, and why the original founders of the FED saw their program of debt-backed security as a hybrid step up—from storing gold bars in a musty old basement, and worrying about a conquering army taking it.

This philosophy of debt-based currency versus a gold/silver-based currency was for sure an improvement *in theory*.

A simple 1 or 2% income tax and federally backed bonds, backed by the taxes of the citizens, or full faith of the US Government, was a profound improvement when the citizens were the government: millions of small businesses and manufacturing plants at the turn of the century, producing products that were known the world over for quality. A small income tax to back our great nation's efforts to build roads and bridges, dams, schools, ship building yards, and power plants seemed reasonable.

But now, trillions of dollars are just Xs and Os on a stream in *the Cloud*. We have 25% of Americans out of work and over 30% working for an ever-growing bureaucracy, or on a pension that is eating up the assets of those who have managed to accumulate something.

In this high tech world where all currency is merely an image on a screen, there is nothing there in many cases. Futures are valued for what might be. And, as inflation swells—no matter how absurd a price we place on something—chances are that in time, if we achieve that price as the dollar shrinks (thereby creating the illusion of profit), that *profit* will then be taxed, reducing the perceived gain.

Enter into this mix, the EPM (electromagnetic pulse), a weapon that we have, Russia has, China has and Israel too. Doesn't hurt anybody, doesn't explode, has no chemical or biological component, just a pulse, a simple energy pulse that wipes out all that data like the wave that swept the Mediterranean and swallowed the great library at Alexandria. We have lots of enemies, most that are politicians in Washington, brought on in our quest for oil. There are others that still carry a banner from ages ago, and they will not sleep or stop.

The balance between good resource management and outright resource abuse has had a profound effect on our nation and its ability to survive. Right now, critical parts of our electrical grid system are no longer manufactured in our country. These parts need a ten to twelve-month delivery window for replacement. All of our fluid systems (oil, gas, water) run on computer-based flow programs that instantly monitor changes in volumes or demands.

Government reports conclude that as much as 90% of the US population would die without water and electricity if an EMP strike takes out our grid controls.

Our banking system would suffer the same fate, but faster. All notes, debts, bonds etc. would simply be in purgatory up in *the Cloud*. The chaos that would follow would be far worse than if we had a bi-metal currency, with the backing safely stored in Fort Knox or in the basement of the Bank of Hawaii (which is where, for some reason, a lot of our gold is). There was a lot stored in the basement of the World Trade Center, too; it was never recovered. I would see who bought a big boat on that cleanup crew.

My point here is that Triumph, to me, is like a little canary in the coal mine. A dot on the world scale, but large enough to support a respectable stream for a 30 or 40-year work cycle.

Yet the people who live in Triumph, the surrounding county, the state, and those in the federal government, would rather do nothing. They would prefer instead to use debt-backed state or federal dollars to just hold the site and bar anyone from it. When gold begins to climb again (and it will), things will require a fresh look. Right now, every time I fire up my little machine, the phone rings down at the courthouse.

As for the plug...Rob Hanson is a good man and the head of the Idaho Department of Environmental Quality (IDEQ). He has a tiger by the tail with this plug. When you vibrate cement in a form, there is a tool used that's a cable in a hard rubber core with a weight at the end, a vibrator. This tool takes the stiffest of cements and allows the aggregates to flow like liquid, filling all the voids in the forms. Well, I think the red iron slimes behind the tunnel plug will act like grease in an earthquake. With 127 lbs. per square foot of water pressure behind it, it will cause the karst rock on the Silver Crown claim to flow like mud. The national Geologic maps show hundreds of earthquakes in our area over the years, and the earth shakes just like that vibrator. It isn't a matter of if it could happen, but when.

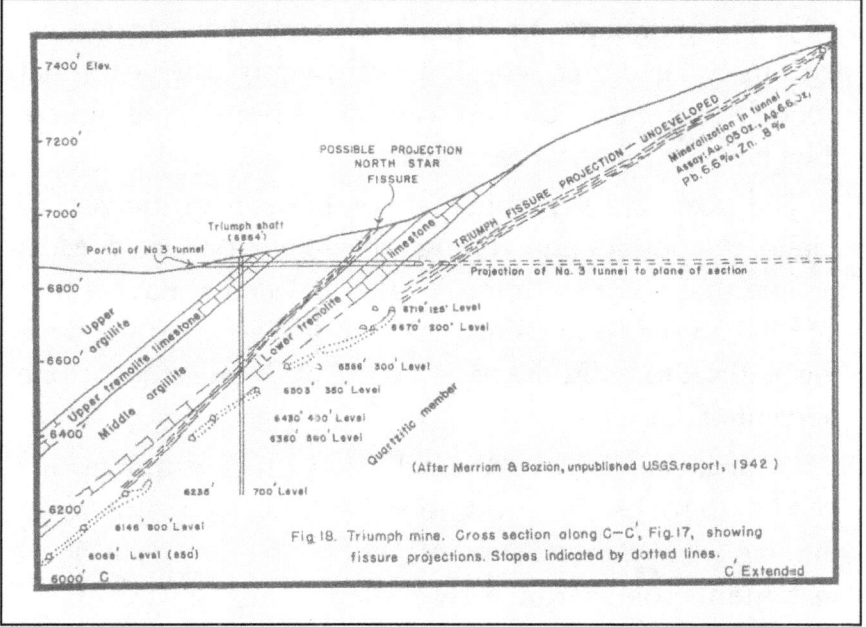

Fig. 18. Triumph mine. Cross section along C—C', Fig. 17, showing fissure projections. Stopes indicated by dotted lines.

It ain't getting no cheaper!

The regulations in Blaine County have gone so extremely far out of whack in just twenty-five years that nobody that has a job here can buy a home here, unless they have an inheritance; nobody.

The taxes are very high in comparison to the rest of Idaho, the politics and zoning are so interconnected. Most people that were ski bums/worker craftsmen have either left, live in public housing, or are in trailers, yet they have the skill set to build the most expensive homes for the one percent of America.

No local resources are used. That's to say timber; it's just left to rot on the forest floor. Few sheep or cattle roam the land anymore. Most of the lamb served at local restaurants comes from New Zealand.

A high percentage of homes in the working class sections are underwater and most people have lost much of their net worth since the 2008 market crash.

Yet, local government continues to assess builders and taxpayers for public housing projects that are *green* and *very* expensive, over $300 per square foot.

There is no sense of fair or right versus wrong here, just the complete and total control of private property rights. Yet people don't fight it for fear of reprisal. This is exactly what happened in Austria in the late 1930s, a slow erosion of individual rights for the common good, one rule at a time. This kind of socialism is a disease that just grows, one layer at a time, until people forget what freedom is. You can always find some asshole developer who provides an argument for this kind of draconian planning. But people need a place to live, and most young couples today are saddled with so many more regulations than we were in the '70s.

Then there's the social fabric itself, pressing down on the family unit. People don't need help, they need to be left alone. Children need to learn more than environmental policy. They need to learn how to build a home, maintain it, grow food, and care for animals.

Now, doesn't it seem just a bit self-centered as a nation to sit on your iPad complaining about chemistry, pollution, and mining, when your iPad is full of the ingredients that, one way or another, came out of the earth?

This kind of simple 4-H agrarian thinking is what our nation was built on, thrift, husbandry, caring for the land from a production point of view, not leaving it fallow in a fairy tale world where wild willows take over and our food supply comes from 4,000 miles away. This is a completely false pretense, and not sound environmental policy but exactly the opposite.

Everyone who grew up in Blaine County or has been here since the '70s, like me, knows what's happened here is wrong, a complete absurdity of policy. Yet nobody sounds an alarm. No new people or development means more room on the mountain, less skiers. That's good.

There was a terrific book, though a bit wacky, called *The Return of the Dove* by Margaret Storm published in 1959. It's the story of Nikola Tesla.

Now Margaret was a devoted New Ager and just like Vernet Harr, Milton's wife, she talked directly with the saucers. The whole Sedona-Findhorn bunch believe that they are helping to hold this giant spinning rock with a burning liquid outer core and solid inner core together, regulating earth's magnetic field, on its god-given path in the universe.

My mother just believes in her Rosary beads, but I think Margaret had the hots for Nicky T, and made him out to be a God in her book. Ole Nick was without a doubt smarter than the average bear, but Tom Edison was no fool himself.

As a boy growing up in Clifton, New Jersey, we would go to the Edison Lab in South Orange. I have returned many times over the years. Getting to see the workshop of a successful industrialist is like going into a time machine.

Edison understood finance in a way I would describe as *New England Thrift* or *The Classic Austrian* School. He understood that if you want to electrify the world, and he clearly did, you have to control it, meter it, sell it, and collect the money. Tesla thought it should be free.

Let's say you had a bakery on the corner and you sold puffed pastry and hot coffee. Things are going pretty well and you begin to get busy, so you hire some dude from a French pastry college who really improves your formula so it's even better. People love it, but at the end of the month, you find out that he has been using real butter, extra cream and expensive honey, so when you pay your material bills, you've made no profit. You will soon be out of business and become a beggar.

Edison was tight as a tack and he had a sign-out sheet at the tool shop window for every wrench, screwdriver, threader, you name it. He was a penny pincher and he had volumes of all available USGS reports on all the minerals and raw materials available in his day. He knew that to run and monitor electricity over every road and backwater in America was going to take millions of tons of wire, and billions of power poles. Tesla saw electricity moving through the air like Wi-Fi. In truth, they were both right.

When our government found itself up against Japan and Germany, they brought in our best and brightest to *the Manhattan Project*. Everyone knows and loves Albert Einstein, but my favorite character from that movie was Farringdon Daniels. He was a nuke guy too, and quickly predicted that the monster they'd created was going to be a problem.

But let me digress. Let's go back to 12th century Christendom. Luigi has his wheat farm and he gets a little drunk at the cantina one night. He leaves his wagon out in the rain. The wheat that was on its way to the miller gets a little wet and a mold grows on it. The mold gets into the flour, and the flour gets into a cake at the church social. Voila! Everybody's tripping, because the mold on that wheat is like LSD. They all see the virgin mother, and the Pope has to figure out what to do about it. The Pope, who is a busy guy and has no time to screw around with a bunch of nut job village women, decides to make all the flour milled in Christendom milled by priests or monks. It would just be easier and make a few bucks on the side, same with the whole kosher thing. Because there's always some stupid asshole who is going to screw up the food supply and people will get sick.

Back to AC power; if every Tom, Dick, and Harry was making electricity we would have total chaos. Could you imagine the morning news? House fires, children electrocuted, get real people. It needs to be controlled by some kind of entity. Now don't get me wrong please; if you're off the grid and you're making power, it's your right. As long as you don't burn down the world around you, go for it. But to force the power companies to buy back a few KW's and feed it back into their grid is ridiculous. They are spending billions on line repair, poll truck convoys, and co-operative disaster relief after tornados and ice events. And then their workers get pensions, health care, and sick pay. Why should they be forced to buy my extra electricity? It just raises the cost for the folks that can't afford, or have no desire, to lay out 30 grand for panels. This a kind of abstract socialism, where a group with the best of intentions hog-ties the very power companies that keep their lights on, until they have to buckle to the real plan, which is a Federal Power Company that dictates more and more to its customers how to live in a perfect world. Meanwhile, the brothers in the hood are scabbing free power right off the pole. I've seen it in Philly.

But now, with the whole Global Warming-One World Government movement, electricity has taken a huge political turn into your home. If you want to build a new home and want the privilege of having electricity, you need to meet the new energy code and have walls of R50. R50!!! That's 4.5 times the insulation of a 1950s house.

That means the lumber bill will be three times higher, the windows will cost three times more, the wire and switches, breakers, doors. All more, much, much, more, and you will need to pay additional fees for a licensed energy auditor. Who the fuck can afford that? Nobody, except trust-funders. A young couple can barely buy pampers and formula. We are systematically handcuffing our next generation, yet they have all been brainwashed in school that they need to recycle and be green.

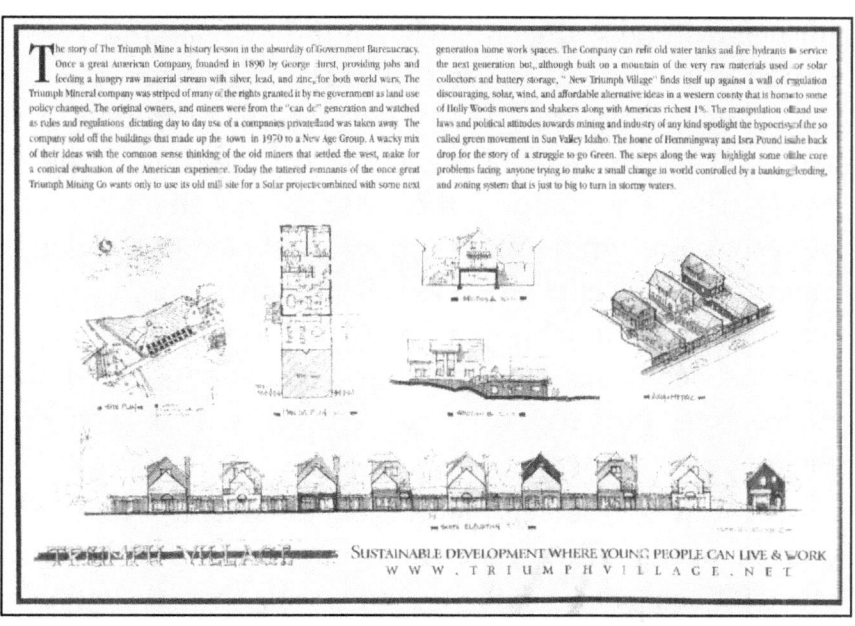

SUSTAINABLE DEVELOPMENT WHERE YOUNG PEOPLE CAN LIVE & WORK
WWW.TRIUMPHVILLAGE.NET

On to Triumph Village.

Milton Harr started Triumph, Inc., with a clear understanding of what his utopia would be. Back in the Sixties, there were lots of communes and drop-out-of-society kinds of places. History is littered with new starts gone bad, from the Massachusetts Bay Colony to early pre–Boar War, South Africa.

The people who moved into Triumph have not only thrown Milton's dream away, but have let the earth swallow them up in an attempt to appear nature conscious. They are letting the wetland surround the town, all the result of beavers, the scourge of the rodent world. They are pumping their sewage into this wetland, but when the community tank was installed, the swamp around town was not flooded. It's kind of like having a leak in your plumbing that you're just too busy to fix, so you just let it slowly ruin your floor and your whole house rots, but you don't care because you plan on moving soon anyway.

Governing yourself takes work, debate, and an occasional fight. But at the end of the day, if people can't talk and take care of their own camp, then they don't deserve freedom.

There are currently a handful of state, federal, and county agencies with their hooks in Triumph, including actions by the ASARCO settlement.

There's the looming issue of the plug... So why, you might say, would anyone want to live there, or worse yet, develop there?

For me the answer is clear. There are resources there that can provide a good living for many years if the right foundation is laid to not only recover them, but utilize them wisely. Also in my opinion, East Fork is one of the most beautiful places on earth. There is no reason, except for outright narrow-minded stupidity, that the mine water and the tailings could not provide a positive income to people and not continue to be a tax drain for the state.

As a nation, we cannot continue to spend fiat currency on government jobs, supported by pensions, for much longer. The castle is made of sand and the rest of the world now knows it. I don't think China will be manipulated by Western banks forever. They will solve their pollution problem when they want to, because they are driven. We are self-destructing from within, just like so many empires before us.

Concerning the mine water.

If you have ever been in a large, commercial greenhouse, you have seen just how hard people work inside. They're potting by the thousands, seeding, making sales, and checking weather. It's a full-time job, and the expensive part of the system is heating, cooling, and water. One could find dirt and mulch anywhere.

The wastewater emanating from the Triumph mine is considered polluted. It is full of red iron oxide, iron sulfate, silver sulfate, and oxidized traces of everything else in the Triumph mineral makeup. It comes out of the earth at 55 degrees and is now running into a settling pond, then running down the hill into private land. The fences and pipe that were put in place from the 1993 clean up are falling down. The settling pond that started clear is now red, and the red iron oxide is begining to move down the rip rap ditch that was created at a considerable expense in the *cleanup*.

When I first came to Triumph in 1974, there was a wooden flume that ran down the hill from the main portal. This flume was built with 2 x 10 lumber, and had several wooden head gates that allowed the water to be diverted to the mill if needed. The iron would build up on the surface of the wood and become very thick, four or five inches, and you could take a square-point shovel and scrape it from the top down. There would be a great pile of oxide at the bottom.

I took a sample of this material to paint manufacturers and brick manufacturers. I traveled to visit the famous architect, Polo Soleri, in Arizona who had a green pigment from a tunnel on his property and tried to trade with him. The trace elements of arsenic in the oxide render it worthless for paint, yet it would work as an excellent mildewcide.

Our EPA rules on paints are so complicated that costs for paint are going through the roof, yet the complicated chemical formulations created to replace the trace elements that were previously put in paint as a mildewcide are, possibly, far more dangerous.

The ingredient SKANE M-8 has replaced lead as a mildewcide and has been linked to beehive collapse; look it up. The glycerides and water-soluble chemicals in water-based paint go into the water and don't come out. They become part of our food chain easier than the old oil-base formulations and every chemist in the business knows it.

A mildewcide is a mineral put into coatings that prevents that green stuff from growing on your house. Prior to 1974, a trace amount of lead, mercury, or arsenic would be added to the batch. After 1974, they were removed and listed as toxic. Then there were lawsuits from poor mothers living in old tenements in Baltimore that found the landlord guilty of exposing the children in his rentals to lead. This was the crack in the dike. Since then, case upon case has found its way through the courts. And American highway bridges have become too expensive to paint, so they are falling apart.

The world's greatest structures have always been protected by coatings formulated using minerals that resist boring insects, rot, mildew, and the elements. Almost all these formulations, standard in *The National Chemical Formulary*, are now being tossed for new ones with complicated proprietary replacements owned by DuPont, Bayer, BASF, or Dow.

Who has this served? It has not served the owners of American real estate, who now have to wonder if their home is safe. It has not served the taxpayer, who sees the cost of painting a public bridge or water tower skyrocket into the stratosphere, so much that bridges are sitting around rusting because the cost of compliance for a simple paint job is astronomical. If that mother in Baltimore and her ambulance-chasing attorney would have just cleaned the house and vacuumed, things may have been different.

Many of the buildings in the US, almost 40%, were built before 1974 and these laws have stolen equity from those homeowners, banks, schools. The costs are very, very high to comply with asbestos and lead paint abatement. But more importantly, they have shown us that the American home is under attack. When you can pass a law on one product and reach back in time, then you can do that with anything. Formica, construction glue, chip board, plastic water pipe, the products are endless.

In one generation, you can use a certain material. In the next it might not only be out of fashion, but be listed as toxic, and need to be removed by a specially trained abatement expert who completed a four-day seminar. He can now charge you $45 bucks an hour, but needs to remove his moon suit and respirator every three hours to have a cigarette. Get the fuck out of my house!!

In Ed Griffin's book *World Without Cancer,* he discusses this kind of conspiracy prophecy where the large German and Swiss chemical companies set out to control the elements on the periodic table like a big board game to rule the world. Everybody wants to rule the world; when he posed this theory in 1978, people called him a crack pot, health food granola head, just out to sell books. But look what has happened in forty years. You can't turn on a TV without seeing an erectile dysfunction commercial, Zoloft, Celebrex; Roundup, Terminix, on and on.

The laws *have* been slowly manipulated to take control of minerals and make them something that needs to be handled in a moon suit.

I'm almost done with my rant.

People in power can always point to the spill, the BP disaster; shit happens, then there's 9/11 kind of stuff or Pearl Harbor. Consolidation of power always happens in crisis. So where do we go from here? How have I woven this dialogue into an egocentric position?

Well for starters, in Triumph we have a little town of very angry people that was once a home to productive industry; a contributor, however small, to the county, state, and federal coffers. And the citizens that lived there had jobs producing raw materials that went down the industrial supply lines to factories making goods. Those goods generated more tax revenue in the towns where they were made, and on and on. That's all dead, killed by government, controlled by government agencies on various levels that have already sued each other for funds, from one department's budget to another's.

Meanwhile, the taxpaying citizens of the community can't pay much tax because they are not working much. Does this make any sense to anybody?

Every single pretext by which the EPA and DEQ took over control of my company's land and minerals has turned out to be totally and unequivocally bullshit. They told us the Clean Water Act requires the owner of a portal with discharge to pay damages. They denied us permission to clean the water in 1980. Then they said that the pond needed to be re-graded and capped so it doesn't hold water. So they fucked up the tailings with pit run rock and topsoil that will make it more difficult to process, but the real poke in the eye for me is they allowed the residents to dig and maintain ponds adjacent to the very piles they told us they needed to keep dry. I again call this bullshit.

But here is what really worries me, and should worry you too. You can talk to any geologist, water engineer, wetlands biologist, and they will tell you stories of the same draconian waste at their site anywhere in the country. Fleets of government trucks, with computer stations mounted on the consoles like big city cop cars, managing our national parks and state lands, protecting them from us with government printed money; backed up with health care, sick pay, vacation days and a pension. But our kids coming out of college have few job prospects.

Just like Rome, just like Austria, just like every other great empire before us, we are killing ourselves from within. Nikita Khrushchev was right.

So the where does the buck stop? For me, it's on my land, in my back yard. Change by example! Grow it, build it, and take care of it, one stone at a time. Keep the bilges pumping with all their might until the storm passes. The only other option is to abandon ship, and that's not really an option because the world population is clearly exploding.

There's about sixty million in gold and silver in the Triumph tailings. That is not a theory, but a fact. There are now billionaires living up East Fork, and more are moving in. The cement trucks are rolling through town to another 20- or 30,000 square foot home out East Fork Road. There are 90 miles of tunnels. Half are behind that plug, filled up to 270 feet above the plug and 125 psi behind it. There are beaver backing up productive lands all around the village, with the sewage seeping into that water. Change it, one thing at a time. Fix it; it takes work, it takes getting up in the morning and figuring it out. Bickering over control of nothing but a dead carcass in the road like a pack of vultures fixes nothing.

I can envision a simple water filtration system, removing 90% of the oxides, running the cleaner water through a parabola to boil it, make steam, use the hot water for gardens and baths, then run it down the hill and spin a small turbine. But that takes work. Then there's the water rights issue, and money.

Some billionaire will pay for that water right to fill his duck pond. I can envision a very small, clean tailings processing plant that slowly produces gold and silver that would service the debt required to build it, man it, and pay off the bureaucrats who will have their hands out.

More importantly, I see horses on the tailings, and riders in a good quality horse-training arena with the hay coming off the lands that the beaver have taken.

I'm sorry, but I would much rather watch a pretty lady take her pony through its paces than a rodent slapping mud with his tail. Triumph should be a little power house, not a toxic waste zone. It's partly about perception, but it's also about doing, and making opportunities for the next generation. Sure, they will have their struggles and dramas, just like we did. These government agencies and trusts also have to be in the mix to make it work, because they are the law, and you can't fight city hall.

Right now, everyone in this nation knows we are sinking. The liberals on the left blame the top one-percenters. The hard right guys are buying ammo and blaming the liberals. My money is on a systematic revisit to resource management; timber, minerals, farming. If we don't support the raw materials side of our supply line by small businesses, trade groups, 4-H, soil conservation, and minerals recovery, we will have 75% of our population in trailers and living on government-supplied green beans in 20 years. We have 47 % now, but nobody wants to believe it.

The folks in these groups—land trusts, Green Peace, hell, even Ducks Unlimited—have been sold a bill of goods, and now we have to pay that bill. Our government in Washington has been bought; we all know it, and they have slowly taken Cloward-Piven style thinking into our homes. It's okay for two men to shoot up and screw one another, but not in a bedroom with single pane glass and R-13 walls... It all about energy conservation, you see.

Get along little doggie!

There has been a concerted effort to run cows and cowboys out of the West. They just don't have the charm they used to. Cows get fat and crap all over. The deer, elk, and antelope were here first, along with wolves, so they should get the wild lands back. So say the supporters of this thinking, from the decks of their 25,000 square foot mountain retreats in Aspen, Vail, Park City, or Sun Valley.

On the surface, these new folks are like me, raised in the East, but so was the great grandpa of every Western rancher.

Why is it that this invasion of western ethics is spawned from the cocktail parties of the premier western ski areas? Why can't they just be satisfied to ski and ride bikes in the summer?

In Zermatt, Switzerland, the queen mother of all ski areas, they run cows on the slopes all summer. They put those great bells on them. Maybe our cows need bells. Then, to beat all, they bring the cows right into town for the winter and put them in little quaint barns next to $300 per night rooms. The smell is supposed to add to the ambiance, and in some ways it does, right down the street from the cheese shop.

It's getting hard to understand where the American mind is headed. We are systematically turning on Aunt

Bee and Mayberry, as if something dark and dirty was going on in the back alleys. Now we have to root it out and put an end to the *American Dream* once and for all. It has always been easy to kill *God, Guts, and Glory* in long periods of peace. It's when the shit hits the proverbial fan, when a population that has been too comfortable squabbling over the finer cuts of meat is staring down the columns of approaching armies, they look to the miners for steel. This is where we are, a whole generation has somehow been taught to undo rather than improve on the foundations set by their fathers. Is that overstatment? Maybe, but China and India are leapfrogging over us by sending their children to our schools, and taking ideas from our companies. They're doing it with our devalued dollars, while our children, the children of those rich ranchers, are having a hard time finding 150 grand for a degree in a field, only to find that the best jobs back in their old Western homeland are for big oil, or the government. I don't need a well-educated statistician to make a power point chart to show me where that's going.

John Muir, Satan or Saint?

We often see glowing PBS productions on the National Park system that place John Muir up on a giant living wooden pedestal, hands outstretched like Jesus, light emanating from his fingertips, in a pose of radiant benevolence. I think that is total bullshit. Let's take a look.

In 1677, in London, there was this document circulating called *The Confession of Faith* and it lumbered on about Jesus and the Trinity, lots of old Testament stuff. Then just to keep the party going, it proclaimed the Pope to be the Anti-Christ.

Now that wasn't nice, and this of course stemmed from that horny old dude Henry, who was banging as many maidens in his court as he could and whacking the heads off of the wives who bore him a couple of female children. And that pesky ole devil Pope wouldn't grant him a divorce. Who did he think he was?

Well, John Muir's dad, a young Scotsman, grew up in the smoke of this religious revolution. He forced little John to memorize the whole damn Bible. Boy, that must have been fun. Then his dad moved to Pennsylvania, because the Church of Scotland wasn't strict enough. Daddy was subjected to these very strict absurdities, only to watch England come in and take his ancestral land, evict its people, ship them off to the American

Appalachian South, and cut down every damn tree in the forest for wooden ships and lumber.

Muir grew big enough to leave home and say good riddance to his nut job parents. He got a job in, you guessed it, the lumber mill.

He travels and writes his way from sawmill job to sawmill job, covering forests from British Columbia to Florida. He even built a water-powered mill along the way.

His distorted, radical religious roots pulled a one-eighty and his personal inner-self just called a big time out on logging, milling, building, and grazing. He just wanted to be still.

His boss, Mr. Pinchot, promoted the sustainable use of managed forest and mineral resources.

"No, no..." said young Muir, "God has spoken to me and we must save, as in do nothing with, vast parts of America—and save them for future minions of retired trust funders who, like me, don't want to work on daddy's farm no more..."

You see, I'm a nobody here, and Mr. Muir has been elevated to a level of sainthood, while Mr. Pinchot is portrayed as clear cutting his way to the coast. But that was not it at all, and the end result created lots of unintended consequences, as often happens.

The national forest I see, when I look out from my perch on the side of the Triumph Mine, is waiting to burn. Then the blackened, charred shafts will stand rotting on their stumps, waiting for new seedlings to replace them in fifty-year cycles of burn, rot, grow. All this is being protected by an army of government paid and pensioned workers, many carrying sidearms, and enforcing rules and regulations that neither Mr. Muir nor Mr. Pinchot could have ever dreamed possible, particularly growing up just a few generations from doctrines like *The Confession of Faith* or *The Toleration Act*.

In my most humble opinion, there has never really been a successful separation of church and state, just a constant ever-flowing river of conflict, created by those in the population who are governed by their self-imposed piety. Is that pious? Um, could be.

Wagons Ho!

About the parade; once a year, the doors of Ore Wagon's garage are pulled open, the horses are trailered in and teamed up, the crowds gather on Main Street and the glory days of the Old West are relived. Afterward, the restaurants are filled with affluent transplants that discuss the marvel of a large wagon and team. It is as if we glorify what we put to death—like a bullfight, or patron saint, or even the big guy himself.

The economy in Blaine County now is just trust fund driven. This was predicted years back, but now it's full blown; all wonderful folks, the children of successful parents or old Uncle Joe who developed some algorithm that paid out big, and now that same driven energy will be channeled to further refine or impose this new doctrine.

The children of the Ketchum School recently petitioned the city council to not allow the circus in town. Now think about that tectonic shift for just a moment and let it settle in.

"But Toby Tyler was coming to town, Mamma..." said little Tim.

"Toby Tyler is a fool," said his mother. "He is just as dumb as the horse he rode in on. You're going to Berkeley like I did."

So the next day at school, little Tim agrees with his indoctrinated classmates: "The circus is a tool of evil capitalists."

Back in Connecticut, the ground trembles as great grandpa rolls over in his grave. But children, like the children of Nazi Germany, or the last Emperor, even Caesar, have often shown just how smart they are by forsaking the 'wisdom' of their fathers.

Utopia with a job. I can see several nightmare scenarios that put us further down that chart of great nations to hale from, if we continue down this path of debt and short-sighted gains.

I can also dream of a day when a new small village of Triumph produces a payout from our mineral dump lasting for a fifty-year cycle, while building a horse or sports center on the tails. This pipe dream is a variation on Rupert's. But there will be a dozen groups, both federal and nonprofits, that will mock my plan. The swamp waters will continue to rise around the village of Triumph, when the fact is, for around $15,000, you could rent a long arm excavator for a month and make a pond deep enough and clean enough to raise trout in, swim in, and skate on in the winter. This could lower the water table by around eight feet and allow the septic tanks to drain properly. By the time the engineers weigh in, there would be another $200,000 in studies and legal fees. Our ship, as a village, as a city, as a state, and as a nation is just floundering, obviously, I find it sad.

The premier western states, Idaho, Utah, Montana, Colorado and New Mexico, have been refranchised by the likes of Ted Turner's, Bill Gates's and the Allen

Companies' guests lists, by what some are calling the one-percenters.

Under the guise of saving the wilderness, they have supported, and in some case started, nonprofit groups that have driven off the middle and lower class ranch families, and turned most of the ski towns into liberal political machines that dictate to state capitals what to do and how to do it. J.R. Simplot was the first I noticed to see the future of western politics, and he pulled out to Canada for the construction of the company's newest and largest potato plant.

It takes a bullet.

Call of the Wild was one of the first books I read that I just couldn't put down. I imagined myself living in the wilderness with a pack of loyal dogs, a fantasy I eventually lived out in Triumph. Satchmo was the best dog one could ever hope to have, a pure white German Shepherd who listened and was fiercely loyal. I took his cousin Luke from a man who was going through a nasty divorce, and for a few years I lived in a shack on East Fork with my horse and two, big white dogs. I feed them meat that I would get from the dumpster at the Triple S Grocery in Hailey on Sunday nights. They would clean out the meat counter and throw everything away. I would often get whole cases of freezer-burned chicken and steaks that were just a little green. '*Hallelujah*, I'm a bum' was my creed, and those were good years. I was young and strong.

Luke was a killer though, and as much as I tried to school him otherwise, he just was. When the sheep would come through East Fork, he would go wild. I would see him in the pack, white on white, causing havoc. Satchy would just sit back and watch. Luke tried to kill horses, too.

One time, I went into Sun Valley with my old mountain horse to sell him to Max Kimble's hack line. I needed the money as a down payment on my first 6x6 GI truck... I was very poor, just barely making ends meet and I rode over the hill from Triumph to Elk Horn, then through Saddle Road and over to the stable that was just north of Ketchum. I bedded down for the night in the tack shed with my dog pack outside.

There were about 75 head of horses in a large corral. At dawn, I awoke to a ruckus in the corral. A mare had lain down to give birth, and Luke was right there doing what killers do at the smell of blood, trying to pull the foal out by the head with his mouth so he could eat it. He put out the young foal's eye, and I put a bullet in Luke's head. I was not going to get paid for my horse. I was not going to get my 6x6 truck. I'd had enough of Luke and his murderous ways.

That was forty years ago. If I did that now, I would be on Animal Planet and they would shoot me, or fine me and garnish my wages for life. I don't hunt, but I don't begrudge people who do. I don't even fish, but the costs of all these agency arguments regarding animal ethics, wolf lovers against cattle ranchers, has become so incredibly burdensome. It's pulling tax dollars away from schools and programs that we need to make better young people.

The gray wolf was happily living in the cold Canadian North. He was not endangered up there, living amongst the caribou herds. To bring him back, noble as the intentions were, this has caused a range war and the two groups will not back down.

The groups are *city people* (that have an income from city sources, i.e.: stocks, bonds, pensions or trusts) versus *country people* who need the land to live. The rest of the arguments are secondary. We are self-destructing, turning on each other while jobs are leaving our country. The rest of the world is laughing at us. We are spending more on dog food, pet care, and animal rights than we spend on our children.

The trend in big cities now for young gang bangers is a *home invasion*. For those of you who have not experienced the home invasion phenomena, a young teen trying to get into a gang will kick down your door, enter your home in the middle of the *Dancing With the Stars* finals, put a gun to your head, demand your car keys, your money, credit cards, and maybe your daughter. Now, that's pretty bad, that's a whole lot worse than young Don Corleone stealing a carpet to take home for his wife.

But here's where it gets real scary for me. That sonofabitch that just pulled this off will get a state supplied attorney, because he is a 'victim of society' and came from a broken home, is troubled, and was under the influence of his drug addiction; he will get counseling.

Just like the wolves, we have become so compassionate that we are protecting our predators, and we are doing it with our tax dollars. So I ask you, who is more dangerous—the predator or the society that protects him? I think this is a weakness on our part, and our enemies on the world stage see it.

And Jesus said, "Turn the other cheek."

Let's put on our cone heads for just a minute. First, I want to call some, and I emphasize *some*, parts of the environmental movement a *white washed wall*.

When a rancher places his flock or herd on land for a hundred years, they have gained a certain precedence. It's true that in the 1700s there were more predatory animals such as wolves, mountain lions, and even native peoples. But, you could make a claim that 300,000 years ago, there were woolly mammoths roaming the western plains, and dinosaurs before that.

But if, in the Buddhist and Judeo-Christian traditions, all of God's creatures—beasts of the field and birds of the air—are equal, then I ask you, in what Biblical interpretation of Matthew, Mark and Paul is it fair to the sheep and cattle to introduce the grey wolf back into territory that was free of them? How can a shepherd honestly steward his flock, knowing that his neighbor has supported and facilitated the reintroduction of a predatory species whose goal in life is to kill and eat the youngest and oldest of all the herds, wild and domestic?

Here we have strayed far from the Covenant, and if there's one thing the Old Testament is good at, it's livestock mediation. Five thousand years of sheep, goats, and cows roaming the Holy Land brings up plenty of case law that has been ignored by an over-educated, and in some cases atheist, judiciary.

Perhaps I have offended my atheist pals, and I love you and appreciate your position. We could point to the Judeo-Christian bankers that have rolled us into war upon war for furs, gold, timber, and most recently coal and oil, and soon rare earths. Who could argue that? But how crazy is it to purposely put the Fox in the hen house, and then spend so much money and time fighting in the courts to defend the Fox, instead of spending money on more productive jobs that add to the GNP of the land?

Tourism is a total dead end street if the population in the cities are faced with ever-increasing food, housing, and fuel bills.

They can't get to see Old Faithful this year, and that's the top draw! There are hundreds of thousands of other beautiful acres of federal land that see very little traffic at all.

So how is funding coming down the pike for all of this without cleaning out the middle class? When the music stops, and it will, the richest 1% of Americans will be held up in the ski resorts of America, with water for the golf courses. And the children of the middle class will be swept off the ladder, held up in new urban environments where all people, of all races, colors, and creeds, will be equally stagnant, idling, with nowhere to go. Because all the production, worker bee jobs are in Asia; and the door on that bank swings one way.

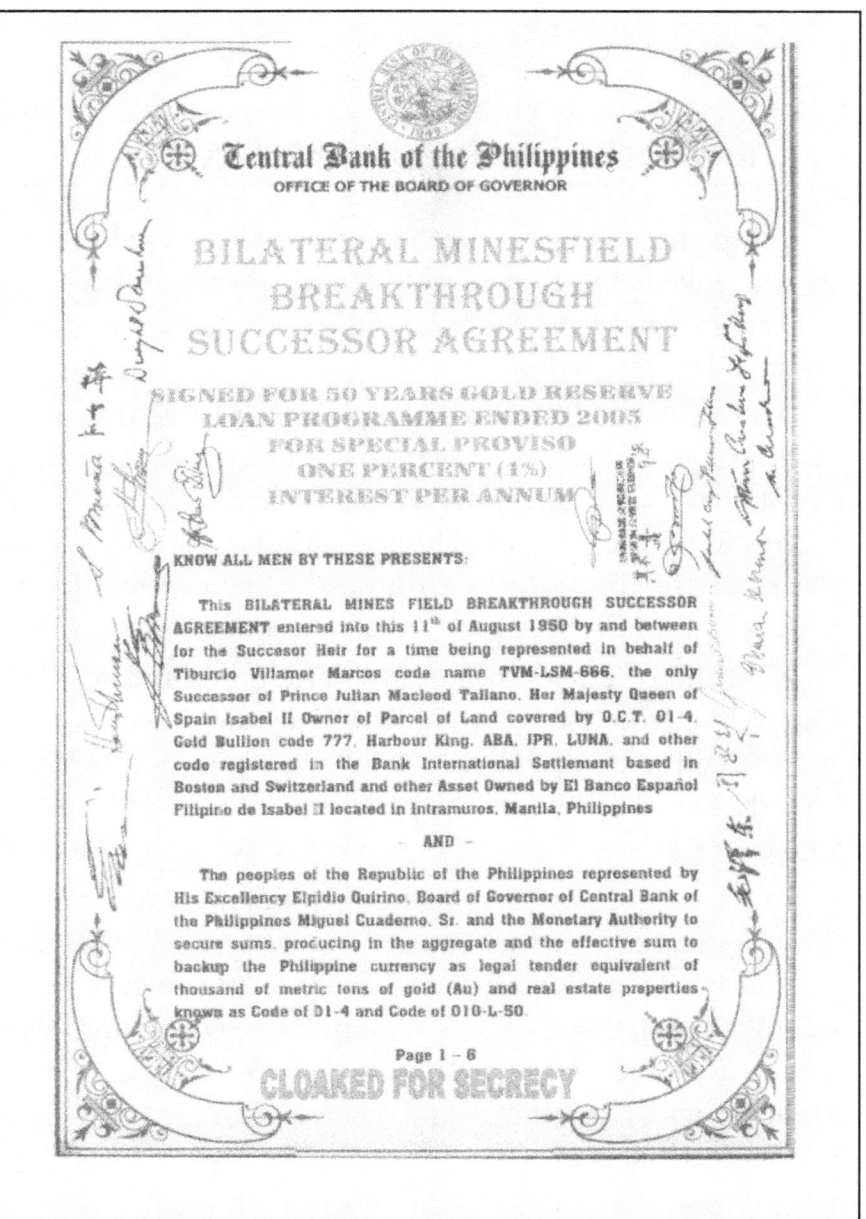

Is the World Bank gold backed?

Europe has held gold for thousands of years: gold from Egypt, taken by Rome, gold from Persia, taken by Alexander, gold from the Incas, taken by Spain, gold from Spain, taken by England.

Well in 1944, Hitler was taking all of it he could steal, including teeth filled with it from the dead bodies he was heaping up. The European Allies moved a lot of it to Hong Kong, thinking the Huns couldn't get it there. But the Japanese got it, along with all they could steal from the millions of Chinese they looted and slaughtered.

As we, our fathers, began to retake the islands of the Pacific, the Japanese had to hide it. They did, in caves and tunnels in the Philippines. In 1949, we found it, lots of it, 150,000 tons, and the world powers had it melted down into bars.

So the world powers, including China, entered into a 55-year financial agreement, a kind of jointly held CD backed by 3.5 trillion 1949 dollars or 150,000 metric tons of bullion, deposited in UBS, Union Bank Switzerland, the same guys that were trading with IG Farben, "Time Honored and Trusted."

The documents were signed by a "Who's Who" of world powers: Ike, Queen Isabela, Mow, Truman, MacArthur, Marcos. They struck "the Bilateral Minefield Agreement." Now there are those that claim this conspiracy a total fraud. But there is a seed of truth in this one, and after all the pilfering and skimming, the foundations of the New World Order were established and "the Order" is Gold Backed.

This massive amount of *blood gold* was the foundation of the World Bank and the United Nations, and it was supposed to be used to help the world, devastated by war. The struggle over its control continues.

When we talk about a gold-backed currency, the one-world dollar that the most powerful players are already using, is essentially the main currency of the world; it is backed by that blood gold in a basement vault somewhere. It's probably back in the Alps where it was held before WW2. Like it or not, we already have the one world order, so we better get used to it.

We are now moving currency so quickly around the globe that the leakage alone is creating inflation. We are still somewhat backed by gold; the notes are not, but the roots of the system are. If the *Cloud* was to be whipped away by a weapon, EMP, or a sun spot, the 4 horsemen are holding gold; so is China. Last year they purchased 160 tons, and they are sitting on a lot in Mongolia at Turquoise Hill.

At the end of the day, all the machinery, and buildings, and broken backs of miners toiling for thousands of years, amounts to pallets of that golden metal, sitting in storage under guard in cement bunkers.

Bonnie and Rupert

In Closing.

As the noose gets tighter in Triumph, we now have a dozen groups with a vested interest in control of the surrounding property of the mine, in the river and the forest. We have wolves living in the 90 miles of tunnels.

The property costs of the homes there are approaching $200,000 for land and old shacks that were built with the company sawmill for practically nothing. But the new rules to replace a little shack make its value ridiculously inflated.

What we have done by making laws more and more restrictive is elevate the value of little 800 square foot shacks, because to build a new one, you can't use local materials; you can't cut corners to get a roof over your head before winter sets in and you and your loved ones freeze. You can't build it as you have the money; you must either have all the money, lots of it, or go into a long-term debt instrument, a mortgage that locks you in 30 years. That's about half of the average adult life. Welcome to 1984, it's here; and it is really more restrictive than Mr. Orwell predicted, but with the advent of smart phones, we are pacified.

By 2084, most of the small farms will be gone. There will be larger garden-type operations, but food supply will be corporate. Health care and population will be controlled. We will probably have a world currency, and we will still be a predominantly carbon-based society, but the oil will come from, shale, coal, ethanol, and natural gas. There will be some electric cars and mass transit, but the raw materials production for batteries is just not enough to put the bulk of our population on the road. By then, China will dwarf us in almost all ways, including freedom.

I hope I'm wrong. But like Rupert used to say as he dug through the earth with his light fastened to his hard hat like a battery-powered third eye: "You can't know where you're going, if you don't know where you've been."

I will look to the future and wait.

Rupe and the Vault

www.ingramcontent.com/pod-product-compliance
Lightning Source LLC
Chambersburg PA
CBHW070527100726
47907CB00004B/1016